Cupcakes and Casualties

A
Peridale Cafe
MYSTERY

AGATHA FROST

For questions and comments about this book, please contact
pinktreepublishing@gmail.com

www.pinktreepublishing.com
www.agathafrost.com

Edited by Keri Lierman and Karen Sellers

ISBN: 9781980657224
Imprint: Independently published

ALSO BY AGATHA FROST

The Scarlet Cove Series
Dead in the Water
Castle on the Hill
Stroke of Death

The Peridale Café Series
Pancakes and Corpses
Lemonade and Lies
Doughnuts and Deception
Chocolate Cake and Chaos
Shortbread and Sorrow
Espresso and Evil
Macarons and Mayhem
Fruit Cake and Fear
Birthday Cake and Bodies
Gingerbread and Ghosts
Cupcakes and Casualties
Blueberry Muffins and Misfortune

A Peridale Cafe MYSTERY

Book Eleven

CHAPTER 1

J ulia South loved the way her pearl engagement ring caught the light as she flicked through a bridal magazine by the window in her café. She was barely paying attention to the dresses on show, her eyes instead on the glittering pearl in the middle of the silver band.

"What about this one?" Sue, her sister, asked as she spun the magazine around on the table. "This is really pretty."

"Maybe for someone half my age," Julia replied quickly. "I'm two years off forty, and that's backless."

"So?" Sue said with a heavy sigh. "You haven't liked any of them."

"It's not my first time going down the aisle," Julia reminded her. "I want something classic and timeless. Something just like Mum's dress."

"This one?" Sue stabbed her finger down on a beautiful figure-hugging dress worn by an equally beautiful slender model in her twenties.

"Maybe if I lost a stone," Julia said with a chuckle. "Actually, make that two."

"Why don't we join the slimming club together?" Sue said as she patted her almost flat stomach. "I feel so fat since the twins were born."

Julia arched a brow, wondering if her sister was serious. She peered into the pram where her two-month-old nieces, Pearl and Dottie, were sleeping soundly. If Julia had not been there when the babies had been born on Christmas Day, she would not have thought they were Sue's. Her body had 'snapped back', which according to their gran, was a trait of all South women. Julia thought it had more to do with her sister being only a few weeks away from her thirty-third birthday, and if Julia ever got pregnant, she would balloon to the size of a house and stay that way until her dying breath.

"You're already back in your old clothes," Julia said as she reached for the last piece of her cream and jam scone. "If I lost some weight, I'd instantly go out of business. Nobody in Peridale would believe I'm still sampling my cakes before selling them. They say never trust a skinny chef, but *I* say never trust a skinny baker."

Sue pursed her lips as she turned to the next page in the magazine. She snapped it shut and turned it over. There was a glossy advertisement for a film on the back. The red-headed woman in the advert looked vaguely familiar, and Julia was sure she had seen her in something before, not that she could remember her name.

"You've got cream on your chin," Sue said as she stood up. "I should go home before these two wake up. I can feel a feed coming on. They don't tell you about the sixth sense you develop when you become a mother, but I just know when they're about to get hungry."

"I'll take your word for it," Julia said before leaning into the pram to kiss her sleeping nieces on their foreheads. "I want a cuddle next time. They're always asleep when you come and see me."

"Because it's the only time of day I get any peace," Sue said with an exhausted chuckle. "I had to buy industrial strength under-eye concealer to stop people from asking if I was '*coping*'."

"Well, your big sister thinks you're coping just fine," Julia said as she kissed her on the cheek. "Maybe Gran was right when she said one baby felt like one, but two felt like twenty."

"Make that twenty-*thousand*." Sue waved as she headed to the door. "You've still got cream on your chin."

Julia wiped off the cream in the reflection of a spoon. As she closed the half a dozen bridal magazines Sue had brought with her, Julia looked around her empty café.

February had always been an uncertain month for her business. Sometimes, spring started early and brought beautiful weather, but more often than not, it was the second-coming of winter before the daffodils blossomed. The year had already brought hail, snow, and enough rain to feed the lawns of the village for the coming decade. Looking out of the window at the clear blue sky and the vibrant village green, it was easy to pretend it was not bitterly cold thanks to the protection of the café's radiators.

After scooping up the magazines, Julia walked

through to the kitchen. She had thought the quiet month would be a good time to start putting together ideas for the wedding, but it was proving to be more complicated than she remembered. The whole event was beginning to feel like a giant house falling from the sky to land on her at any minute.

"Whatever happened to simple?" she mused as she flicked through one of the magazines on the stainless-steel counter in the middle of the kitchen. "None of these dresses will suit me."

She landed on a page Sue had ear-marked. It depicted a model closer to her age than most of the women in the magazine. She was slightly shorter than the others too, but she was still incredibly slim. Julia turned to the fridge and assessed her blurry reflection in its shiny surface. She held the magazine up beside her and breathed in as far as she could.

In her flared 1940s-style black dress with its flattering waistline and covered shoulders, she looked slimmer than she knew she was underneath it. She had been a slim child and even a slim young adult, but every year, usually around Christmas, she gained a couple of pounds. To reflect that, her dress size had slowly crept up, making her two sizes bigger than she had been on her thirtieth birthday.

"What are you doing?" a voice asked from

behind, startling her.

Letting go of her breath, Julia spun around to see her foster daughter, Jessie, parting the pink beads into the kitchen, a confused look on her youthful face.

"Do you think I should lose weight for the wedding?" Julia asked as she looked at the picture again. "Not a lot, just a little bit."

"Why?" Jessie asked, arching a brow as she tucked her hands into her black hoody pocket. "You look normal."

"*Bride* normal, or *normal* woman normal?"

"*Huh?*"

"Do you think I'd suit this dress?"

Jessie looked down at the picture in the magazine. She gave her shoulders a shrug, her dark eyes as uninterested as Julia should have expected from a seventeen-year-old girl more comfortable in baggy black clothes and Doc Martens than dresses.

"Wedding dresses look dumb," Jessie offered as she scratched the back of her dark hair. "Why do you care so much?"

"Because the photographs last forever," Julia said as she stared blankly at the beaming model in the magazine. "Ignore me. I'm being silly."

Jessie squinted and looked down her nose in the

way only she could. It only lasted a second before she shrugged again and set off across the kitchen to the white boxes on the side.

"Are they all correctly labelled?" Jessie asked, her tone switching from '*teenager*' to '*adult*'. "You mixed up Evelyn's fairy cupcakes with Shilpa's red velvets."

"I'm sure they didn't mind."

"That's *not* the point," Jessie snapped. "It's *my* name on the label, not yours."

Julia looked at the colourful '*Jessie's Cupcakes on Wheels*' logo that they had designed and made into stickers for the cake boxes. When Jessie had come to Julia with the idea of starting a cupcake delivery business to tide them over in the quiet winter months, she had thought it was a brilliant idea.

Since then, Jessie had been taking the venture seriously, and to Julia's surprise, it had taken on legs of its own. What she had thought would start as Jessie riding around on her bike dropping off the odd cupcake here and there had resulted in orders coming in thick and fast. With the cold weather keeping people in their homes, Julia was glad her cakes were still being enjoyed around the village, and she was also pleased that it was helping the café's bank account even after Jessie had taken her cut.

"Double checked," Julia said with a wink. "I can

triple check if you want, boss?"

"I'll take your word for it," Jessie said as she stacked the boxes. "If the orders keep coming in like this, the bike basket won't be big enough. I'll have to start taking your car."

"Pass your test, and I'll happily let you," Julia said with a pat on Jessie's shoulder. "But until then, we'll keep the roads of Peridale safe."

"The test guy was an idiot!" Jessie cried with a roll of her eyes. "He should have been more specific when he said, '*follow that car*'. I didn't know he wanted me to stop at the lights."

"The light was on red."

"I was paying attention to the car!"

"And the other five tests?"

"Not my fault."

"I'm sure you'll make a great driver," Julia assured her as Jessie headed back to the beads. "But until then, it's the bike!"

Jessie mumbled something under her breath as she headed for the café door. Julia chuckled to herself as she gathered up the bridal magazines. She had lived with Jessie long enough to know that teenage mood swings made it impossible to guess which Jessie she would get from hour to hour.

She looked down at the happy women on the

covers. The only thing stopping her putting the magazines in the bin was knowing how much Sue had paid for each of them.

"They're models," she reminded herself as she tucked them away in a drawer. "Women paid to look beautiful and sell me a lie."

When Julia closed the drawer, her fiancé, Barker Brown, walked into the café. He was wearing his usual detective inspector suit, but it was missing the usual tie, which she quickly noticed was clutched in his fist.

"I'm officially off for two weeks!" he exclaimed as he tossed the tie onto the nearest table. "If the station calls, I'm not answering."

"Chocolate cake to celebrate?" Julia asked, already taking a slice of Barker's favourite from the display case. "Do you think I should lose some weight?"

Barker lowered himself into the chair nearest the counter, a sceptical look on his face. His lips parted to reply, but the words did not form.

"I feel like that's a trick question," he said finally as he accepted the chocolate cake. "You look perfect as you are."

"Perfect enough for the wedding?"

"Whose wedding?" Barker mumbled through a

mouthful of cake.

"*Ours!*" Julia said, holding up her pearl engagement ring. "Unless you're retracting your Christmas Day proposal?"

"Oh," Barker chuckled, spilling crumbs down the front of his white shirt. "Why would you want to lose weight for that?"

"Because brides are beautiful."

Barker's eyes widened as he munched another mouthful of cake. Julia walked back to the counter and plopped a peppermint and liquorice teabag into a cup before filling it with hot water. After making Barker his usual Americano with an extra shot, she sat across from him, the models on her mind.

"Are you trying to insinuate that you're *not* beautiful?" Barker asked, a dark brow arching up his forehead. "You're the most beautiful woman I've ever met, Julia South."

"Love is blind."

"And so are you if you think you need to lose weight," Barker replied with a roll of his eyes that reminded her of Jessie. "Is this that sister of yours? Has she been whispering in your ear again?"

Julia did not say anything, but she knew her face gave it away. She blew on the hot surface of the tea to disguise her blushing.

"You're perfect," Barker said. "And you'd still be perfect if you doubled - no - *tripled* in size. Do you think I really care about that?"

Julia shrugged, knowing full well he did not care about such trivial things, but also unable to take her mind off the brides in the magazines.

"Well, I don't," Barker said before licking the chocolate icing off his lips. "If anyone needs to diet, it's me. I think your gran was right about me getting soft around the middle. I blame your cakes."

"I'm not forcing you to eat them."

"But you'd be upset if I didn't," Barker whispered as he leaned across the table to kiss her gently on the lips. "You've got cream on your chin."

Julia picked up Barker's chocolate-covered knife to use as a mirror, a speck of the cream on her chin having evaded her previous attempt to wipe it away. She rubbed until her chin turned bright red.

"Ignore Sue," Barker said as he leaned back in the chair before unbuttoning his shirt collar. "You look normal."

"Bride normal or normal woman normal?"

"Huh?"

"Never mind," Julia said with a shake of her head, her chocolatey curls springing free of her ears. "Any plans for your two weeks off?"

Before Barker could answer, the roaring of an engine caught their attention. They turned to the window and watched as a giant yellow digger rolled past the village green, followed by a truck carrying a giant skip. The convoy crawled towards the opening of the lane leading up to Julia's cottage before disappearing from view.

"Looks like they're knocking down what's left of my cottage today," Barker said as he wiped his finger along the crumbs on the plate. "I wonder who the mystery buyer is."

Five months had passed since a violent storm had destroyed Barker's cottage, forcing him to move in with Julia further up the lane. In that time, he had been trying to sell the ruins without much success until a mystery buyer reached out through their lawyers. The offer had been low, but Barker had bitten their hands off just to offload the property. The money from the sale had been enough to pay off the mortgage, leaving Barker with a couple of thousand pounds to put aside into his savings.

In the weeks since the sale, the gossip channels had talked of little else. That chatter had only intensified when plans for a modern redevelopment had surfaced, prompting a taskforce of locals under the collective name of '*The Peridale Preservation*

Society' to start a petition. Many of those in the group, including Julia's gran, put part of the blame on Barker, not that he had known what was to become of his cottage when he sold it.

"Why don't we go away this weekend?" Barker suggested. "We could get the train down to London and soak up the sights. We could even catch a show."

"What about the café?"

"I'm sure Jessie can handle it," Barker said, grabbing her hands across the table. "She's been whizzing around on that bike like the Wicked Witch of the West for weeks. She might enjoy standing behind the counter again. Just say yes. It will be fun!"

Before Julia could agree to anything, Evelyn Wood, the eccentric owner of the local B&B, floated into the café in a bright yellow kaftan.

"Spring is coming!" she announced airily. "I asked the spirits for good weather, and they have delivered as usual."

"Why didn't you ask for good weather when it was snowing last week?" Barker asked with a tight smile. "I'll leave you ladies to it. I won't take no for an answer, Julia, so get Jessie on board."

Barker kissed Julia on the cheek, nodded to

Evelyn, and grabbed his tie before heading out of the café.

"Sounds ominous," Evelyn whispered as she adjusted her matching yellow turban. "Are things okay at home? If the energy is off, I can come and sage it for you."

"Barker wants to take me on a weekend trip to London," Julia said as she cleared away the plate. "But I appreciate the offer."

"Oh, how *wonderful!*" Evelyn exclaimed, clapping her hands together. "I foresaw good news for a close friend in the cards this morning. You *must* go! It's been so long since I've been able to get to London, so you will have to tell me all about it. Alas, it looks like I will be kept busy for the coming months, what with my B&B being fully booked for the first time since the summer."

"What spell did you cast to make that happen?" Julia asked as she looked around her café, which was noticeably lacking the usual tourists from the warm months. "It's been like a ghost town in here."

"Then I come with good tidings!" Evelyn exclaimed, clapping her hands together again. "The builders developing Barker's old cottage are all staying at my B&B for at least the next eight weeks, but it could be longer if the snow returns. However,

I shall think of their time and not my own greed, and I will pray for constant sunshine."

"How many builders?" Julia asked, the cogs in her mind already ticking.

"*Ten*!" Evelyn announced brightly. "Ten strapping men, all of whom will have large appetites after a day of building."

"And during," Julia said, pulling her supplier book from under the counter. "If I put on a lunch menu, do you think they'll come?"

"Of course!" Evelyn cried. "I'm providing breakfast and an evening meal, so lunch is all yours! Give me some business cards, and I'll pass them on."

"I could get a chalkboard sign for outside," Julia said, her eyes glazing over as she handed a small stack of cards to Evelyn. "This is perfect. Ten, you say? How many slices of bacon do you think that will be a week?"

Evelyn counted on her hands for a moment but gave up almost instantly. She chuckled and shrugged, instead choosing to clutch the crystal hanging around her neck.

"I'm a vegetarian," she said, almost apologetically. "Never eaten the stuff."

"I'll just order a lot," Julia said. "You said you came here on business?"

"Ah, yes!" Evelyn exclaimed. "With the men staying for such a long time, I wanted to give them some home comforts. I thought about baking some cakes myself, but I realised I could never match your ability. You *are* the best baker in Peridale, after all. I thought you could drop a cake by a couple of times a week. Something big enough to feed ten men, but I'll leave the flavours up to you. I'll pay you, of course."

"I'd be more than happy to," Julia said, scribbling down what Evelyn had said. "I'll give you a discount for ordering so many. And, if you get them all in here for lunch tomorrow, the first cake is on me."

"Then it's a deal!" Evelyn cried as she pocketed the business cards somewhere in her kaftan. "And say '*yes*' to Barker! You'll have a wonderful time in London." Evelyn paused and looked Julia up and down, her finger tapping on her chin. "I must say, Julia, you look especially beautiful today. I'd kill for a figure like yours."

Julia looked down at herself. She could feel her cheeks blushing for being silly enough to take Sue's slimming club comments to heart.

Evelyn turned to leave just as a motorbike pulled up outside. A leather-clad figure stepped off before pulling back a black helmet to reveal a handsome man in his late twenties. He had messy dark hair tucked behind his ears and a black nose-ring in his left nostril. Julia even spotted a tattoo of a red rose creeping above the collar of his jacket and onto his neck. He looked up at the café sign before pushing on the door.

"Hello," he said, a kind smile stretching his mouth widely as he looked around the café. "Cute place. I think I'm a little lost. This is Peridale, right?"

The stranger pulled off his gloves to reveal that the tattoos crept down his hands and all the way to his knuckles.

"It certainly is," Julia said as she assessed the stranger who looked oddly familiar. "Can I get you a drink?"

"I'm actually looking for the B&B," he said, hooking a thumb over his shoulder to the motorbike. "I'm here for a building job."

"Say no more!" Evelyn exclaimed, immediately rushing to the handsome stranger's side, her arm looping around his. "We might have spoken on the phone. I'm Evelyn, and -"

Evelyn's voice trailed off as she dragged the stranger out of the café, leaving his motorbike still parked outside. Julia found herself staring at it for what felt like a lifetime, sure she had seen the man somewhere before but unable to pinpoint where exactly.

Turning her mind to Evelyn's compliment of her figure, Julia fished the magazines out of the drawer and placed them on the counter. She flicked through one of them again, slightly more optimistic than she had been when looking through them with Sue. When she landed on a simple white dress with lace sleeves and a neat train, she managed to visualise herself in it, and she liked what she saw. Closing the magazine, she tossed it onto the counter, but it bounced onto the floor, landing face down. She picked it up, the advertisement for the film that had caught her eye earlier shining up at her. It looked like a cheesy romantic comedy; something Julia would probably enjoy but not openly admit to liking. The familiar-looking redheaded actress in the middle of the advertisement was perhaps a similar age to Julia, but more beautiful than any of the models inside the magazine. She had a natural smile that was warm and inviting, and a jawline so tight it could cut stone.

"I bet you've never worried about your figure," Julia whispered to the paper woman.

She placed the magazine on the counter just as a man and a woman walked in. She thought she had at last been sent some customers, but when her eyes landed on the woman's face, Julia blinked hard, sure she was seeing double. She looked down at the magazine advertisement, and then up at the woman, her soft face and vibrant hair the exact same. The woman was on the phone, chatting away at a hundred miles an hour, while the short and slightly plump bespectacled man stayed in her shadow, two large bags on each shoulder.

"Did you see a digger go past here?" asked the woman sharply, barely looking at Julia as she kept her phone to her ear. "I can't get my bearings. I'm looking for Thorn Cottage - well - what's left of it."

Julia looked down at the magazine, and then up at the woman again; they were the same person.

"Are you -"

"Candy Bennett?" the woman replied, a smile pricking the corners of her lips. "Would you like me to sign your magazine?"

Without waiting for Julia to respond, she passed the phone to the man and then clicked her fingers repeatedly until he produced a marker pen from one of the bags. Barely looking at the magazine, she scribbled her signature under the image of herself.

"Thorn Cottage?" she asked again, this time making brief eye contact with Julia, her lips lacking the easy, warm smile in the glossy image below. "We're in a hurry."

"Just up there," Julia said, pointing to the opening of the lane as she blinked away her confusion. "I can show you if you like? I live up there too."

"No need," Candy replied, passing the pen back to the man and then snapping her fingers until he replaced it with the phone. "I guess that makes us neighbours."

With that, she turned on her high heels and strutted back to the door. The short man struggled with the bags before adjusting his glasses and flashing Julia an apologetic smile. She waited for the door to close behind them before grabbing her phone.

"*Sue?*" she whispered down the handset as she looked at the signature on the glossy advert. "You're *never* going to believe who just came into my café."

CHAPTER 2

Wrapped up in her thickest coat, Julia looked on as the team of builders chatted in a circle next to the giant digger. A thermos of tea made its way around the group as the tall bald man she suspected to be in charge ran through the itinerary for the day.

Despite the early morning chill and the grey clouds circling above, a small crowd had formed on the road outside the half-destroyed cottage. The residents of Peridale were nosier than most, but Julia knew even they would not be that interested in watching a demolition. As it happened, she was not the only resident to have come into contact with Candy Bennett. Word of the actress' arrival had whipped around the village in record time, with at least eight people telephoning Julia to check that she had heard '*the news*'.

"An actress in our village!" exclaimed Shilpa Patil, the owner of the post office, her breath steaming the air as her lips chattered. "I've never heard of her, but my Jayesh says she is a big deal."

"She was in one of the soaps for years," Evelyn said, a heavy wool blanket wrapped around her white kaftan. "She was killed off rather unceremoniously in an off-screen car accident."

"I heard she left to focus on films," added Amy Clark, the church organist. "I think I saw her in something at the cinema once."

Julia wondered if it was the same film she had seen her in. After a little online research, she had managed to pin down where she had seen Candy's face. It had been in a romantic comedy she had seen on a rare trip to the cinema five years ago. She remembered enjoying the film, and according to the facts she had read online, it was a role that had earned Candy a handful of awards. As of late, Candy had been taking more theatre work, but in a recent interview, she insisted that she was being '*selective*' about the roles she agreed to because she wanted to '*enjoy*' acting again.

"Did I miss it?" Sue cried as she hurried up the lane with the pram. "Is she here yet?"

It was rare that Sue wasn't dolled up, but she looked extraordinarily glamorous for half past seven in the morning.

"That's a lot of perfume," Jessie coughed as she wafted her hand in front of her face. "Did you fall in a flowerbed on your way here?"

"It's *Chanel*," Sue said, holding her wrist out for Julia to sniff, even though she could smell it before Sue had even reached them. "It's expensive."

"Trying to impress someone?" Barker asked as he bent over to say hello to the twins, who were both awake and looking up at the sky with their crystal blue eyes. "Which one is which?"

"Pearl has a freckle under her left eye," Sue said as she gave her wrists a cautionary sniff. "If it weren't for that freckle, I'd still have no idea myself. They're like clones. Is she here yet?"

"Who?" Jessie asked, barely looking up from her phone as her thumbs typed rapidly. "The Queen?"

"*Candy*!" Sue cried as she straightened up her blouse. "She'll appreciate my taste in perfume. I usually save it for special occasions."

"I didn't realise you were so enthusiastic about demolitions," Barker said as he rubbed his fingers across Pearl's red cheeks.

"I'm not," Sue said with a wave of her hand. "But I intend on making Candy my best friend. If there's a famous actress in the village, I want first dibs."

"She's not *that* famous," Jessie mumbled with a roll of her eyes. "I've never heard of her."

The conversation died down as the cold set in. The sun had barely risen, but it did not stop people arriving from every direction. After ten minutes passed, Julia was sure she saw every recognisable face in the village standing on the tiny lane outside Barker's old cottage.

"Here comes trouble," Barker whispered to Julia as he nodded down the lane. "I'm just glad I'm not on duty today."

Julia craned her neck to see her gran, Dot, along with half a dozen other residents in t-shirts with '*Preserve Peridale's History*' emblazoned proudly across their chests. Harriet Barnes, their leader, and the woman who had started the petition group from her florist shop on Mulberry Lane, was marching at the front of the group with a placard exclaiming that they should '*STOP GENTRIFICATION*'.

"*People of Peridale*!" Harriet called out, her voice travelling without the aid of a microphone. "We beg you to join us to stop this *illegal* demolition of a listed building! This piece of history should *not* be destroyed to make way for a holiday home for an actress who does not care about our village or its people."

Julia saw some people nodding their heads in agreement, but most looked disinterested and resumed looking out for the arrival of Candy. Dot waved to Julia, an excited grin on her face. She had already admitted to Julia that she did not care much for the cause she was protesting, but she enjoyed shouting in a group, especially if they had their own printed t-shirts.

"*People of Peridale*!" Harriet exclaimed again. "I *implore* you to halt this demolition. If we surround their equipment peacefully, they cannot carry out their illegal work. This building should be *restored*, not *destroyed*."

"There's not much of a building left to restore," Shilpa whispered in Julia's ear. "Is she seeing what we're seeing?"

Julia shrugged as she looked at the half-shell of Barker's cottage. The storm had caused a massive telegraph pole to crash into the sitting room of the cottage, taking out most of the dining room with it too. The bedroom and bathroom were untouched, but a large portion of the exposed cottage had been weathered by the elements. If the remainder of the building was to be saved, there would not be much left to rebuild from.

"This building dates back to the 1700s!" Harriet cried. "Much like most of Peridale, our style and values have not changed since then. Why are we allowing them to build a *hideous* glass and steel structure in our *fine* and *traditional* village?"

Another wave of chatter echoed through the group, but no one rushed forward to surround the equipment as Harriet had instructed. The builders, who had been watching in amusement, began to laugh, their bald leader laughing the loudest as though mocking the group.

"*People of Peri -*"

But Harriet's cry was cut off by the roar of a car engine as a black Range Rover made its way down the lane, slowing to a halt on the other side of the crowd. The chatter grew, with many of the younger residents pulling out their phones to capture the arrival of the car.

"That's *her*!" Sue cried as she readjusted her hair. "It *has* to be!"

The driver's door opened and the short, bespectacled man who had been in Julia's café yesterday jumped down. A groan of disappointment shuddered through the crowd. The man ran to the passenger side and opened the door. He held out a hand, and like an angel floating down from the clouds, Candy Bennett slid out of the car. She was even more beautiful than Julia remembered. In a cream trench coat nipped in at the waist with a belt and skin-tight black jeans coupled with high heels, she looked every inch the famous actress. The small man smoothed out her red hair before applying a yellow hardhat, which looked more like a prop from a film set than a piece of actual safety equipment.

As though the crowd had not watched her getting ready, Candy turned around and applied the same smile from the advertisement on the back of the bridal magazine. She waved at the crowd, and she was immediately met with rapturous applause and flashing of camera lights on dozens of phones.

"Do not worship this *false* idol!" Harriet exclaimed over the crowd. "She is here to *deceive* and *betray* us! She is *not* one of us!"

AGATHA FROST

Candy glided over to the gate, the crowd parting around her like the Red Sea around Moses. The man scurried behind, opening the gate for her. She maintained the same smile until her back was to the crowd, but Julia spotted the corners of her mouth drop immediately.

"She's so beautiful," Sue whispered, her teeth biting her lip. "How do I get close to her?"

"This is *illegal!*" Harriet screeched, running towards the gate with her placard, the rest of her protest group hurrying behind her. "You do not have the permits to do this! This is a listed building!"

Harriet reached out for the gate, but Candy held up her hand. As though she had just been hypnotised, Harriet let go of the gate and stepped back. Candy smiled again, clasping her hands together as she looked out at the crowd.

"I can assure you, we have the necessary permits to proceed with this build," she said, a sweetness to her voice that had been absent when Julia had first met her. "Harold, show this nice lady the papers."

Candy snapped her fingers at the man, who fumbled with his bag to pull out a piece of paper. He hurried forward and handed it to Harriet, who snatched it from him.

"But this is -"

"Impossible?" Candy jumped in. "I can assure you, it isn't. The council agreed with me that this building was beyond repair and it would be better for all to build something new and worthy on the land. Listed or not, some things cannot be fixed. Every detail of our plan has been checked, double-checked, and approved. Nothing illegal is going on here."

"Then you *bribed* them!" Harriet cried, turning back to the crowd. "Don't believe this woman! She's an *actress*! She's a paid *liar*! She's come to Peridale to use our village as her holiday spot in the country."

"I can assure you, I am one of you now," Candy called out, her soft voice floating effortlessly above the noise. "This protest is nothing more than a hysterical cry to cling onto the past, when the truth is, any one of these protestors could have bought this cottage to restore it, but did they?"

Candy folded her arms as she waited for a response. A couple of the protestors dropped their heads, but none of them answered. Julia caught Dot's eye, who seemed to be revelling in the unfolding drama.

"*Girls!*" Harriet cried, tossing the paper to the floor. "As we planned!"

In the blink of an eye, Harriet ripped open the

gate and sprinted towards the digger, followed by Dot and another of the protestors who produced chains and padlocks from their bags. Harriet climbed into the mouth of the digger with the nimbleness of a woman half her age. Dot and the other protestor attempted to chain her up, but they were batted away by the tall, bald builder. As though she weighed no more than a bag of cement powder, the builder scooped her up and tossed her over his shoulder.

"Might I remind you all, this is private property," Candy called out, her tone stern over Harriet's screams of outrage. "I will not call the police on this occasion but let this be a warning to any other daring protestors - I *will not* tolerate trespassers!"

The builder put Harriet on the ground, her grey hair breaking free of the two pencils that held it up in a bun behind her head. He held her arms behind her back as she thrashed and cried out.

"What do you want me to do with her, boss?" the builder asked, his accent gruff and Northern. "I think you should have her booked."

Candy considered his suggestion for a moment, but she shook her head and lifted a hand.

"A warning is enough for now, Shane," Candy

said with a firm nod. "Do you understand, lady?"

Harriet brushed her silver hair from her face as she looked up at the actress, who seemed to have grown an extra foot over the course of the interaction. Harriet nodded feebly, her yelling already a distant memory.

Candy walked forward and shook Harriet's hand, and as she did, Harold appeared out of nowhere with a camera in his hands. Candy pulled Harriet in, whispered something to her, prompting Harriet to look at the camera with a shaky smile. Candy beamed like in the advertisement again, the camera flashed, and she let go. Shane escorted Harriet off the land, leaving Candy to turn her back on her adoring public. Julia wondered if she was supposed to see the actress squirting hand sanitiser into her palms immediately after.

"Am I late?" a high-pitched male voice cried, forcing all heads to turn down the lane. "I don't want to miss this."

"You're right on time, Mikey," Candy called out, opening the gate for the impossibly slender and smartly dressed man with bleached blond buzz-cut hair. "We're going to build the house just as you designed it. The planning came through as expected this morning. Shane? Get on with it."

Mikey, who Julia assumed was the architect behind the glass and steel house design, linked arms with Candy and they both stepped back and watched as Shane clicked his fingers at the tattooed biker who Julia had also already met. The biker climbed up into the digger, and less than a minute later, they were watching him bring down the head of the digger on the rest of the cottage. Like a hot knife slicing through butter, the bricks crumbled under the weight, sending up a cloud of dust.

"Well, that's that," Barker exclaimed, his fingers clasping around Julia's. "What an eventful morning."

MUCH OF THE CROWD MADE THEIR WAY into the village when they tired of watching the digger scoop rubble into the skip. Luckily for Julia, a large number of those people found their way into her café. After what she was sure had been the busiest day of the year so far, she was happy when closing time neared and the café finally quietened down.

Julia let Jessie finish early, so she could spend some time with her boyfriend, Billy, leaving her alone in the café to bake a cake for the builders at

Evelyn's B&B. She settled on a giant version of Barker's favourite double chocolate fudge cake, which she knew went down a treat with all who tried it.

With the cake boxed up and a tray of leftover lemon drizzle cupcakes from a cancelled order, Julia made her way through the village as the sun started to set. The days had slowly been growing longer, but she was sure today was the first day there had been light in the sky when she locked the café.

Evelyn's B&B sat on the corner next to The Plough pub, down the street from Julia's café. Its garden wrapped around the side of the house and was wildly overgrown, but it suited the look of the tall, stone building. For the first time in months, all of the guest room lights were on, and it warmed Julia to know that Evelyn had a full house again, something she knew she enjoyed. After pulling on the musical chain doorbell, Julia stepped back and waited.

Instead of Evelyn answering the door, her grandson, Mark, answered. Mark had only been in Evelyn's life since the storm that destroyed Barker's cottage had also uncovered a secret basement under Julia's café. The basement had turned out to be concealing the body of Evelyn's daughter, Astrid, who had been missing for two decades. In the event of uncovering the truth behind Astrid's death, Julia had discovered that Astrid had had a son in secret who had been raised by someone else entirely. Knowing she had played a part in reuniting Evelyn with a twenty-year-old grandson she had never known about was one of Julia's proudest moments.

"Oh, hello, Julia," Mark said as he brushed his straightened black hair out of his eyes, which were circled in dark eyeliner. "Is that the cake Nan ordered? She's deep in meditation at the moment. Come in."

After wiping her feet on the doormat, Julia followed Mark into the dimly lit B&B. The scent of burning incense hung thickly in the air, and it was somehow strangely comforting. She enjoyed visiting the B&B. Evelyn was a well-travelled woman who frequently spent the winter months trotting around the globe gathering trinkets for her museum-style décor, but this year she had chosen to stay in Peridale to bond with Mark.

Mark showed Julia into the sitting room, where Evelyn was sitting crossed-legged on the large coffee table in a circle of tea light candles. A low humming came from her throat as she swayed back and forth, but she seemed on an entirely different planet.

"I find it's best to leave her when she's like this," he whispered. "I think she's communicating with my mum."

Julia nodded her understanding as she followed Mark through to the kitchen. She was not sure she believed in the things Evelyn did, but she knew that Evelyn believed, and that was enough for her. They walked into the kitchen, and Mark flicked on the blinding fluorescent lights. Julia placed the cake boxes on the counter where Evelyn had already started to chop vegetables for the evening meal.

"Do you want a cup of tea?" Mark asked, already reaching for a teacup. "Nan ordered some off the internet, and she swears you can see the colours of people's auras if you drink it while the sun is setting."

"None for me," Julia said, holding up her hand, knowing all too well from personal experience what kinds of tea Evelyn liked to collect. "Maybe next time."

"Do you need to be paid for the cake?" Mark asked. "There's some petty cash somewhere."

"First one is on the house," Julia said with a shake of her head. "We have a little deal. How are you enjoying living here?"

"I love it," he said with a shy smile as he flicked

his black hair away from his eyes. "I'm staying in Mum's old room at the top of the house. I haven't changed much about it. It makes me feel connected to her."

A booming voice echoed down the staircase, startling them both. Without a word, they ran through the living room, and past Evelyn, whose rocking had intensified.

Julia reached the foot of the narrow staircase, and she was surprised to see the bald builder, Shane, pinning the tattooed biker up against the wall by his throat. What was even more surprising was that Shane was completely naked from head to toe, his body well-defined and chiselled from years of manual labour, despite looking to be in his forties. The biker, on the other hand, was wearing a white t-shirt and black jeans. Both arms were covered in dark tattoos, and from what Julia could see, it did not look like there was a patch of fresh skin left.

"You tell anyone," Shane cried, his voice booming as he pushed his arm further into the biker's throat, "and I'll *kill* you! You understand me?"

The biker stared at Shane for a moment, his eyes bulging as his face turned bright red. Julia would have run up the stairs to pull the man off him, but his nudity threw her; she did not know where to look. When the biker groaned and nodded, Shane backed away before half-throwing the biker down the stairs. He caught his balance on the bannister before hurrying past them and out of the front door. Shane, who did not seem bothered about his naked state, looked down the stairs, his eyes filled with rage.

"What are you looking at?" Shane cried, his attention focussed on Mark. "Are you queer, or something?"

With that, Shane turned on his heels and marched into the nearest room. He slammed the door so forcefully that Julia felt the floor shake under her feet.

"What was that about?" Julia whispered. "And why was he naked?"

"I - I don't know," Mark mumbled, clearly embarrassed. "He doesn't seem very nice."

"You're right," Julia said, giving his arm a reassuring squeeze. "He doesn't. Ignore him."

At that moment, Evelyn appeared in the doorway, a dreamy and sleepy smile on her face. She blinked slowly at Julia, reminding her of a sloth.

"*Julia!*" Evelyn said airily. "What a lovely surprise. Can I interest you in some of my new tea?"

After declining a second invitation for tea, Julia left the B&B with a promise to return in a couple of days with another cake. When she saw the tattooed biker sitting on the kerb edge visibly shivering, she sat next to him.

"You should have a coat," she remarked. "I'm Julia, by the way. You came into my café yesterday."

"Alfie," he replied through chattering teeth. "You're right. It's freezing."

They shared a laugh for a moment while Julia resisted the urge to reach out and warm his arm with her hand. Being this close to him only intensified the feeling that she was sure she had met the young man before. She glanced over his tattoos, none of which made much sense to her, but she liked them regardless. She was not sure many would suit being so covered but coupled with the nose ring and his dark features, he pulled them off.

"What was that about, Alfie?" Julia asked. "You don't have to tell me, but it looked pretty serious."

"Nothing," he said, forcing himself up off the ground. "You're right. It's too cold to be out here. I'm going back inside."

"Is Shane your boss?"

Alfie looked down at her, and he seemed as though he was going to speak for a moment.

"It doesn't matter," he replied with a distant gaze. "He's a jackass. Wrong place, wrong time."

Without saying another word, Alfie ran back to the B&B door. Julia stood up, the cold starting to seep through her coat. She looked at the front door again, wondering what could have enraged Shane so much that he would put his nudity aside to berate one of his employees.

As though he had just heard his name, Shane burst through the front door, this time fully dressed in faded jeans, a shirt, and a black denim jacket. He hurried past Julia as though she was not there, and made his way towards the pub. He lingered outside for a moment before a taxi pulled up and a hooded figure wearing dark sunglasses climbed out. Instead of going into the pub, they snuck down the alley alongside the building.

Unable to stop herself, Julia hurried down the street so that she could see into the shadowy alley. In the amber glow of the nearby streetlamp, she watched Shane push the stranger up against the wall. Unlike when he had pushed Alfie, his grip was now tender. The stranger who had climbed out of the taxi pulled back their hood to reveal bright red hair. The second they pulled off their sunglasses, passion erupted between them, forcing Julia to hurry down the street.

"Candy Bennett and the *builder*?" Julia mumbled to herself as she made her way to her car parked next to her café. "Stay out of it, Julia. It's none of your business."

CHAPTER 3

J ulia woke up to the scent of bacon tickling her nostrils. She rolled over in bed, her grey Maine Coon, Mowgli, jumping onto the floor. Forcing her eyes open, she saw that she was alone in bed.

"What time is it?" she groaned to Mowgli as he looked up at her from the side of the bed. "Did I sleep through my alarm?"

A quick glance at her blinding phone screen let her know she still had ten minutes left to sleep before she had to get up to start baking for the café. She rolled back over, and almost pulled the covers over her head to enjoy those final minutes of peace, but the bacon smell was too enticing.

In her pink dressing gown and sheepskin slippers, Julia shuffled into the kitchen where Barker, wearing her frilly apron, was hovering over the stove. She watched him for a moment as he wiggled his hips to the song on the radio, unaware of her presence.

"You're up early," Julia muttered, hugging Barker from behind as he flipped the crispy bacon. "I thought you were going to sleep in now that you're not at work?"

"Old habits die hard," he replied. "I wanted to surprise you with breakfast in bed, but you're up now, so sit down and don't lift a finger."

Julia climbed onto the end stool at the breakfast bar, her eyes still half-closed. The sun was struggling to lift its head through the murky clouds outside, letting her know what kind of day it was going to be.

"Extra crispy with plenty of ketchup," Barker said as he placed the bacon sandwich in front of her. "Just how you like it."

"I don't think the slimming club would approve," Julia said as she stared down at the sandwich, her stomach rumbling. "I hear white bread is the devil these days."

"What's life without a little sinning?" Barker shot over his shoulder as he filled the kettle. "I hope you don't still think you need to lose weight for the wedding. I told you, you're perfect as you are, and I won't hear otherwise."

Julia bit into the sandwich, the sweetness of the ketchup mixing perfectly with the saltiness of the bacon and the creaminess of the butter. For now, it tasted too good to give up for the sake of a dress.

"S'good," Julia mumbled through a mouthful as she slopped a tiny blob of ketchup down her dressing gown. "We haven't even set a date yet. There's still time."

"We could always run down to the register office and do it this afternoon?" Barker joked as he glanced at the cat clock above the fridge. "We can take Mowgli as the witness."

"As easy as that sounds, I think my family would kill us."

"Well, since you don't want to do that, and I don't want to get on the bad side of Dot, I might spend the day writing," Barker said, nodding to the dining room where his typewriter lived. "I've had a couple of ideas for the new book. My publisher wants to see a draft of the first chapter before we launch the first book."

Barker had spent most of the previous year writing his first mystery novel, The Girl in the Basement, which he had loosely based on Julia finding Evelyn's daughter underneath her café after the storm. Julia, who had not been allowed to read the book until recently, had thought it would be a passion project for Barker to occupy his time when he was not solving real crimes around the village. She had not expected Barker to find an agent, who in turn had secured a lucrative three-book deal with a major national publisher. Neither Julia nor Barker knew what to expect from the book's release, which was only a couple of months away, but the publisher seemed excited about its chances.

"If it's as brilliant as the first one, you'll do just fine," Julia mumbled through another mouthful of bacon and bread. "I'm excited to read about the continued adventures of Julie North and Robert Greene."

Barker had written Julie North, the plucky café-owning amateur sleuth as an almost identical copy of Julia, but Robert Greene, the new detective inspector in the village of Perington, was younger and taller than Barker and was described as having '*model-like*' features. Barker claimed his publisher had encouraged him to tweak the character to make him more '*appealing*' to readers, but Julia was sure Barker's vanity had played a role in the alterations.

"While we're on the topic of the book," Barker started as he placed a cup of tea in front of Julia. "They want to have a meeting with me this weekend. I know I said I'd take us away somewhere, but I thought we could kill two birds with one stone. Their offices are in London anyway. The meeting shouldn't take too long, and it would be a good chance for you to meet them in person. They're a really cool bunch."

"I haven't agreed to go away yet," Julia said as she wiped ketchup from her chin with a piece of kitchen roll. "With the builders in town, the café is going to be busy. I don't want to leave that on Jessie."

"I've already asked her, and she's fine with it," Barker said with an excited smile as he pulled his laptop from his briefcase. "I've found this gorgeous hotel. They have rooms available for tonight, and they're discounted because of the time of year. We could even get a suite if we're feeling fancy. We'll get the train down after you've finished work, go for a nice meal, have some drinks, and see the sights. I have the meeting tomorrow morning, and then we're free to do whatever we want. I found an app where you can buy last-minute musical tickets. We could see any show you wanted, all on me. I need to spend my book advance on something."

Julia looked at the pictures of the hotel on the laptop. She could immediately tell that it was a five-star from the luxury on display. She thought about her café, and her arrangement with Evelyn to bake cakes, but then she thought about how nice it would be to get away for the weekend and think about nothing other than where to eat and drink in between taking in shows.

"It's tempting," Julia said as she blew on the surface of her tea. "Alright, you've twisted my -"

Before Julia could finish her sentence, a key jangled in the lock of the front door. They exchanged a curious glance before making their way into the hallway. Jessie's alarm clock buzzed in her bedroom, her groan letting them know she was not the one trying to open the door.

"I wonder who that could be?" Barker asked sarcastically. "Shall I make her a cup of tea?"

Dot, the only other person to have a key to the cottage, burst inside in a flurry of icy wind. Her roller-set hair pointed in every direction, and the pleats in her usually pristine skirt bent every which way.

"Morning, Gran," Julia said as she pulled her dressing gown together. "Is the doorbell not working?"

"There's no time for that!" Dot cried, leaping forward and grabbing Julia's pink pea coat from the hat stand. "Put this on. You need to come with me *immediately*!"

"I'm in my pyjamas," Julia said with a laugh as she looked down at her slippers. "What can be so important that I can't get dressed first?"

"I've just found a body!" Dot exclaimed, an eager glint in her eyes. "At the building site! The police haven't even arrived yet."

Julia looked back at the rest of her unfinished bacon sandwich, and then at Barker as he scrolled through the hotel website while the kettle boiled for another cup of tea. Without a second thought, Julia pulled on her coat and followed her gran outside, her curiosity in Dot's wild claims too strong to ignore.

"Why are you up so early?" Julia asked as she struggled to keep up with her nimble gran, who had never let her eighty-four-year-old age slow her down. "The sun is barely up."

"Harriet arranged another protest meeting at the building site before the builders arrived," Dot said quickly as they hurried down the winding lane towards the destroyed cottage. "She wanted to cause some trouble to the equipment as a last-ditch attempt to stop the renovation. Betty arrived just before I did, and we saw the poor fella at the same time. He's lying face down on the rubble, blood all over his scalp. Betty thought he might be a drunk having a nap, but I knew better. The moment we called the police, I ran to get you."

Julia did not need to ask why her gran had thought of her immediately after discovering a body. Julia had earned a reputation for being somewhat of a sleuth in the village over the past year. Whenever there was a mystery to be solved, she somehow found herself mixed up in the middle of it.

The shadow of the tall digger came into view against the backdrop of the milky clouds as they hurried around the bend. Betty Hunter, the sweet owner of the local charity shop, waved to them as they approached. She was wearing her '*Preserve Peridale's History*' t-shirt under her heavy coat and scarf.

"They're still not here yet?" Dot cried as a gust of wind attacked the bottom of Julia's dressing gown. "Cut-back Britain at work!" Dot hurried to the wall and pointed dramatically into the building site. "There he is. Poor guy probably didn't know what was coming his way. That's a murder if ever I saw it."

Julia approached the gate, but she did not reach out to open it. She squinted at the pile of rubble her gran was pointing at. Her stomach flipped when the blood-covered scalp Dot had spoken of jumped out at her. From the black denim jacket and faded jeans, Julia knew exactly who the man was.

"Go and have a look," Dot cried, pushing Julia forward. "Do your thing. Figure it out before the police arrive to really stick it to them!"

"I can't just go wandering around a crime scene," Julia whispered, stepping back from the gate with her hands up. "How do we even know he's dead? Did either of you check on him?"

Betty and Dot exchanged a guilty glance before shaking their heads. Julia sighed, and looked back at the man, wondering if it would be worth checking to see if he had a pulse. The gash in his head seemed pretty deep, and from the amount of blood covering the dusty stone underneath him, it did not look likely that he could have survived whatever had caused the trauma. As though to solidify her thoughts, a black crow flew in from a nearby tree, landing on the body's shoulder. It hopped around for a moment before pecking at the body's ear. Julia clapped her hands to scare the bird away.

"Look at *that*!" Betty cried, pointing at a slab of stone lying in the unattended grass metres away from the body. "It's covered in blood. I'd bet my pension that's the murder weapon!"

"Go on, Julia," Dot whispered, nudging her in the side. "You know you're better at this than any police officer."

Julia was flattered by her gran's praise, but as she stared at the body and then at the lump of stone, she could not bring herself to take another step forward. She dealt with people and facts, not crime scenes and bodies.

"Gran, I -" Julia started, only to be cut off by the blaring sirens of multiple police cars. "Looks like the professionals are here. Maybe we should take a step back."

Dot huffed before reluctantly walking away from the wall. Betty, who could not take her eyes away from the body, joined Dot as two police cars and an ambulance curved around the tight lane. The first police car screeched to a halt in front of the women, and two uniformed officers jumped out.

The second police car parked up behind them, blocking off the lane altogether. Julia's heart sank to the bottom of her stomach when a man she had crossed multiple times climbed out of the car.

"Why am I not surprised to see *you* here?" cried Detective Sergeant John Christie, his eyes zooming in on Julia. "Peridale's very own snoop!"

"Good morning to you too, John," Julia replied with a tight smile. "It was actually my gran who discovered the body. I just happen to live up the lane."

DS Christie narrowed his eyes at Julia, a smirk on his lips. He was a forty-something-year-old colleague and friend of Barker's, but in recent months he had taken exception to Julia's involvement in many high-profile cases, mainly when she solved them before the police had a chance. She was sure the DS was a kind man when he was at home with his wife, but Julia had yet to see a side of him she did not dislike.

"Let's get this over with," DS Christie called to the uniformed officers as he nodded to the gate. "One of you cordon off the scene and the other start looking to see what's gone on here. I don't care which, just get on with it. I want you gloved-up and on high-alert."

The younger of the two officers began wrapping blue and white police tape around the garden wall while the other ventured into the scene. A paramedic ducked under the tape before slowly approaching the body. Under the instruction of DS Christie, they put on a pair of gloves and checked for a pulse. They did not say anything, but the shake of their head and the cold look in their eyes told Julia what she needed to know.

"I'll check his pockets," DS Christie called out as he snapped on a pair of latex gloves himself. "If we can get the John Doe identified before forensics get here, we might get a head start on this one."

"I know who he is," Julia called out, walking up to the tape but not daring to go any further. "His name is Shane. I don't know his surname, but I do know that he's a builder who was working on this site yesterday and that he was staying at Evelyn's B&B."

"And how do you know that?" DS Christie asked with a heavy sigh. "Feminine intuition?"

"Because I have a memory," Julia said, pursing her lips and crossing her arms tightly over her open coat. "I saw him around quarter to six leaving the B&B last night wearing those exact clothes, which tells me he was probably killed sometime before he had a chance to return. I don't care if you don't believe me, but I am right."

DS Christie looked as though he was going to argue, but instead, he crept towards the body. With a touch as light as a feather, he patted down the pockets until he found a wallet in the top pocket of the thick denim jacket. He scanned a plastic card inside before his eyes darted to Julia; she knew she had been right from the irritated look on his face.

"The victim is a Mister Shane Parsons," DS Christie called to one of the young officers who had been making notes in a small pad. "Forty-six years old, and a resident of Burnley, so he's a hundred and something miles away from home. There's also a trade supplier's card for a building company in here, so I'd take a stab in the dark and say he's here with the team of builders staying at the B&B. Bag this up. It could be evidence."

"I told you she was good," Dot whispered to Betty. "She gets her brains from her grandmother. Oh, looks like the cavalry has arrived!"

Julia looked down the lane as the nine other builders walked around the vehicles blocking the road. They were all dressed for a day of work on a cold building site, some of them already wearing their yellow hardhats. Julia spotted Alfie, whose eyes were planted on the ground. He walked separately from the other builders, and he was the only one who was silent.

"Blooming heck!" one of the builders cried in a deep voice. "That's the boss!"

Julia watched as the shock of the scene in front of them washed over the group of burly men. She felt like she was witnessing something that should have been private.

"We should go," Julia whispered to Dot. "This doesn't feel right."

"But it's just starting to get good!" Dot cried, her eyes firmly on the builders as they crowded around the tape. "Start interviewing them. I bet one of them did it! Probably wanted a pay rise. You know what men are like. Think with their fists, not their brains."

"Let's go," Julia repeated out of the corner of her mouth. "This isn't the time *or* the place."

Dot sighed, and with a pout of her lips looped her arm through Betty's before they made their way slowly past the builders.

Julia lingered for a moment and watched as the builders talked amongst themselves while the police officers combed the area behind the tape. It did not take her long to notice that Alfie was no longer with them. She craned her neck around the ambulance just in time to see him vanish around the bend.

Deciding to take her own advice, Julia returned to the cottage where Jessie was finishing what was left of her bacon sandwich. She planted herself on the stool next to her foster daughter and dropped her face into her palms.

"I hope you didn't book that hotel," Julia said to Barker with an apologetic smile as she reached out for her lukewarm tea. "It seems there's been another murder in our fine village."

CHAPTER 4

Rain usually meant Julia's café would be empty until the sun finally came out, but when something big happened in Peridale, a morning of rain would not stop the gossips leaving their houses. Word of Shane's murder spread around the village within an hour. By the time Julia had finished baking a quick batch of chocolate orange cupcakes to have something to sell when she opened up, she already had a line of people waiting at the door.

Julia's café was usually the gossip hub when even mundane things happened in the village. Whenever news of an affair or a divorce whipped around, the gossips came out to voice their opinions in the café. This morning, however, most of her customers seemed more interested in hearing Julia's take on the events since she had been there when the police had arrived. Aside from giving the builder's name and age, Julia bit her tongue and kept the other information to herself. She had, however, scribbled down in her ingredients notepad her recollection of what she had witnessed when visiting Evelyn's B&B, and more importantly, what she had seen in the dark alley next to the pub.

Despite not having any work to do for the day, some of the builders visited the café for their lunch while the others spent it in The Plough. Unlike the residents of Peridale, they were less interested in talking about the gossip and more interested in sampling Julia's new lunch menu. Without needing to pry too hard, it became apparent to Julia that despite their shock surrounding the murder, none of them would be losing sleep over the death of their boss.

"I've worked with him on a couple of jobs before," one of them said through a mouthful of scrambled eggs. "Nasty piece of work."

"Bit too handy with his fists as well," another added. "Once smacked me around the head for accidentally stepping on his shoe."

Julia had a head full of questions she wanted to ask about Shane, but she knew better than to start spouting them in a café full of people. It was better to keep an ear to the ground, and that had already painted a picture of a man she was struggling to find any redeemable qualities in.

After lunch, the builders cleared out of the café, allowing Julia and Jessie to have a quiet couple of minutes to clean the tables before the next wave of customers arrived.

Julia had not expected that next customer to be Candy Bennett, who was followed closely by the short, bespectacled man, who Julia remembered was called Harold. The flamboyant architect, who she also remembered was called Mikey, followed them in. Without asking for permission, Mikey pushed together three of the tables in the middle of the café and began pulling out large blueprint plans and stacks of paperwork.

"We're going to need coffee," Mikey announced

to Julia as Candy and Harold took their seats at the table. "We need to iron out a plan before the day is over."

Mikey collapsed into a seat and dramatically fanned himself with one of the pieces of paper. He had tanned skin and thick, bleached blond hair that had been buzzed to within a couple of millimetres of his scalp. His face was beautiful and chiselled in an androgynous way, with crystal blue eyes and plump red lips. Julia could not tell if he was wearing makeup, or if his sockets and cheekbones were so sharp that they cast their own shadows. Like Candy, his looks were model-perfect, which only made Harold stand out even more. It was not that Harold was unattractive, he actually had a pleasant and kind face that humanised him, but with his thinned hair, glasses, and short stature, he certainly stood out between the two beauties. From the way Julia had witnessed Candy speaking to Harold, she assumed he had some sort of assistant title.

As Julia served the tray of coffees in the middle of the table, she realised she had yet to hear the man say a word.

"This is *highly* inconvenient," Candy cried as she picked up a cup of black coffee while ignoring the milk and sugar. "We're one day in, and we're already behind."

"Not to mention the group is without a leader," Mikey added as he continued to fan himself as though he was in a tropical climate and not an English village on a drizzly day. "Shane might not have been the best with people, but he was the best at what he did. I've worked with him on countless building projects, and he's never once missed a deadline."

"The police are saying it was *murder*!" Candy exclaimed. "Who knows how long this is going to slow us down?"

She paused to sip her black coffee, her eyes flickering slightly as her attention drifted away from the table. Julia wondered if she was thinking about her passionate alley meeting with Shane.

"I spoke to the DS in charge," Mikey said after adding four cubes of sugar to his coffee, his hands shaking. "He wasn't the nicest of men, although he was quite good looking. He thinks we should regain access to the site within the next forty-eight hours."

"Good," Candy said firmly as she placed her cup on the table. "I want this house finished on time. I knew I should have just bought something pre-built."

"But then you wouldn't have had me to design

you the house of your dreams," Mikey said with a wink. "So, every cloud has a silver lining."

The pair let out shrill, fake-sounding laughs that sent chills running down Julia's spine. Harold shifted in his seat, half joining in with the laughter, but looking as uncomfortable as Julia felt. She cast a glance at Jessie, who was staring at the table with wide-eyed bewilderment.

At that moment, Jessie's boyfriend, Billy, returned on the '*Jessie's Cupcakes on Wheels*' bike after having agreed to help out so Jessie could stay at the café during the unexpected morning rush.

"All sent out, Miss S," Billy said with a salute as he walked into the café, barely looking at the trio in the middle of the room. "Any more orders?"

"A couple came in while you were out," Jessie said, already walking through the beads into the kitchen. "I'll get them boxed up."

Billy nodded and lingered by the counter next to Julia. He smiled awkwardly at her while they waited for Jessie to return with the boxes. Billy had once put a brick through Julia's café window, among many of his other petty crimes, but since he had been dating Jessie, he had straightened out his ways. Julia liked the boy, and she often let him put in shifts at the café when she needed an extra pair of hands, for which he was grateful owing to his unsuccessful job hunting.

"If we push everything back by two days, we might be able to claw some extra time if we make them work a couple of Sundays," Mikey announced as he looked over a large spreadsheet. "We'll have to get around some labour laws, but I think a little cash in hand will sweeten the deal."

"Forget the law!" Candy cried. "I want my house finished. You promised me."

"And you'll get it, my dear," Mikey replied with a playful smile. "Something like this isn't going to slow us down. We're still a person down though. I can promote from within to find a new leader, but it means reshuffling everyone. We're going to end up a man short no matter what we do."

"What about the agencies?" Candy asked. "We can get someone, can't we?"

"It will be expensive at this short notice," Mikey said as he flipped through another stack of papers. "We've already wildly overspent in many areas. You wanted the Calacatta marble imported from Italy, and the furniture you've selected won't come cheap. We could always cut corners there and make some swaps?"

"Compromise is always good," Harold said,

finally speaking, his voice deeper and harsher than Julia had expected for such a kind face. "I've been saying that since the beginning."

"I'm not compromising, Harold!" Candy cried, slamming her hand on the counter. "Just find someone, Mikey. If the agency is too expensive, there must be someone in this damn village with some building experience who will work for peanuts. Tell them Candy Bennett will give them a shout-out on bloody Twitter! Do whatever it takes, just don't spend more money."

At that moment, a lightbulb fired above Julia's head. Without taking a second to think about it, she grabbed Billy's shoulders and pushed him forward.

"Billy will do it," Julia exclaimed. "Won't you Billy? You've got building experience, haven't you?"

Billy looked up at Julia with another puzzled look. Julia could sense he was about to protest, so she gently nipped under his arm, causing the expression to vanish.

"Yeah," Billy said, still looking at Julia with a frown. "Plenty of experience."

"How old are you?" Candy asked with an amused look. "Twelve?"

"Just turned eighteen," he said with tension in his jaw. "Do you need the help, or not?"

The beads clattered as Jessie walked back into the café with the labelled boxes. Julia shook her head quickly, letting her know to stay back and not get involved.

"Cash in hand?" Mikey asked quietly, as though he was offering to let Billy into a secret society. "Under the table?"

"Depends how much you're offering," Billy said, stepping forward from Julia, a smug look on his face as he looked down at the paperwork. "My discretion comes at a price, mate."

Mikey and Candy looked at each other before Mikey flicked through the paperwork again. He counted some numbers on his fingers before scribbling something down on a piece of paper and passing it to Candy. She took the pen from him, crossed out whatever he'd written, wrote something else, and gave it back. Mikey nodded and then cleared his throat.

"Forty quid a day," Mikey said, leaning back in his chair to fan himself with the small piece of paper again. "Take it, or leave it, kid."

"Sixty," Billy replied. "I'm not a mug."

Julia stepped forward, but Billy held his hand up. Mikey stared at Billy with a smirk for what felt like an age before turning to Candy; they seemed able to communicate without saying a word to each other.

"Fifty," Mikey countered. "Final offer. Six days a week, for a minimum of eight weeks. If you can figure that out, it's -"

"Two thousand, four hundred quid," Billy announced before Mikey had a chance to finish. "I'd call that a deal."

Billy reached across the table and extended his hand to Mikey who accepted it cautiously. Billy shook it heartily before turning back to Julia with a pleased grin.

"I'm glad Dad was watching that boring business documentary last night," Billy whispered as he winked at Jessie over the counter. "First rule of business is you never take the first offer, or so they kept saying."

"You're full of surprises, Billy Matthews," Julia said as Mikey gathered up his paperwork. "Well done."

"Why d'ya wanna work on a building site?" Jessie asked as she pushed the boxes across counter. "I thought you were going to help me with this?"

"It's two grand, baby," Billy said, an excited quiver in his voice. "Where else am I going to earn money like that? I'll take us on holiday somewhere really classy. Flights to Benidorm are well cheap this time of year."

Billy accepted the boxes of cupcakes, saluted, and made his way back to his bike outside. Candy clicked at Harold until he passed her phone across the table. When they were all packed up, Candy tapped some buttons on the screen before putting the phone to her ear.

"*Katie*?" Candy called down the phone as she walked to the door. "It's me, doll. We're coming back to the manor early. Something happened at the site. I'll tell you when I get there. Shopping trip? Sounds perfect."

With that, the trio left, their coffees barely touched, and the tables left where they had arranged them. As Julia put the café back to normal, she realised they had not even paid.

"I know what you're up to," Jessie announced as she cleaned the table next to Julia. "I bet you pushed Billy forward for that job to be your little mole."

"I don't know what you're talking about," Julia replied with a playful smile as she put the chairs back where they belonged. "But now that I know where the famous Candy Bennett is staying, it seems I'm going to have ears in more than one place."

CHAPTER 5

Saturday passed by uneventfully considering the murder the day before. Since no one actually knew Shane, interest in the crime fizzled out faster than usual.

For Julia, it was all she could think about. Barker left the village for his meeting early Saturday morning, and now that it was no longer a trip for pleasure, he planned to stay until Tuesday evening to cram in as many meetings about the book launch as he could while he was away from the station. Jessie spent her Saturday evening with Billy, leaving Julia alone in her cottage with nothing more than Mowgli, her thoughts, her laptop, and a pen and paper.

Early Sunday morning, the sun finally came out, and the crime scene tape came down, with work on the project resuming on Monday morning according to Billy. It was almost as though nothing had happened.

Later that morning, Julia found herself walking up to Peridale Manor with Sue, Pearl, and Dottie, and a head full of questions.

"I can't believe you organised a playdate without asking me first," Sue grumbled as she forced the large pram over the gravel driveway towards the grand entrance of the manor. "Spending Sunday morning with Katie is not my idea of fun."

"She's our step-mother," Julia said, the words amusing both of them considering Julia and Katie were the same age. "And her baby with our father is our brother, and you know you love Vinnie as much as I do."

"Of course," Sue said as she looked down at Pearl and Dottie, who had somehow slept through the bumpy journey up to the manor. "He's adorable.

His mother, on the other hand, that's a different story."

Their relationship with Katie Wellington-South had been as bumpy as the gravel under their feet. It had been six years since their father had married the young and wealthy ex-model, and for most of those six years, their relationship had been frosty. Over the past year, however, Julia had been working hard to repair their relationship with their father, especially since finding out they were going to have a new baby brother. Along the way, she had discovered that their father and Katie's love was real, that Katie was not so bad under the peroxide hair and revealing outfits, and that they could be a happy family despite their dysfunctional nature.

Sue, on the other hand, had been a little more resistant to the changes. The addition of three new babies to the family had helped heal a lot of the old wounds, but Julia was beginning to think Sue and Katie's personalities were not suited to being friends.

"Why are you so interested in tagging along, anyway?" Sue asked as Julia knocked on the giant oak door. "At this age, they can't even sit up on their own. It'll be like watching giant slugs."

Julia glanced at the black Range Rover parked next to Katie's pink one. She had neglected to mention that Candy Bennett was staying at the manor, although now that she was thinking about it, she was sure an afternoon with the famous actress might have been a more appealing proposition than a playdate.

Hilary, the elderly housekeeper, answered the door. Her white hair was scraped back into a tight bun, her bulging eyes lined with black kohl liner, and she was wearing one of her usual grey cardigans and skirts. The only difference to her look was the cane she now used to walk after having been pushed down the grand staircase on the night of Barker's surprise birthday party that Julia had organised at the manor.

"Oh, hello," she said, her spiky edges softened a little since the fall. "You're early."

Without saying another word, Hilary swung open the door and hobbled to the side to let them in. Since having to learn to walk again, she was slow and cumbersome, but she had worked at the manor for decades and had insisted on staying despite having been offered a healthy retirement package. Her role was now ceremonious rather than practical, with most of the housekeeping duties being passed onto the younger and less experienced staff members who did not seem to stay more than a couple of weeks. Julia wondered if that had something to do with Hilary scaring them away, purposefully or accidentally.

With Julia's help, Sue managed to get the bulky pram over the threshold without waking the twins. Hilary closed the door behind them before leading them towards the sitting room, but Sue stopped in her tracks when she noticed Candy Bennett gliding down the staircase in a white silk dressing gown with a fur collar, cuffs, and trim. Sue opened and closed her mouth like a fish out of water, but she was too star-struck to say a word. Candy reached the bottom of the staircase, barely glancing at the new arrivals. When her gaze flickered over Julia, there was a glimmer of recognition, but she did not say anything before sashaying into the kitchen.

"C-Candy Bennett is staying *here*?" Sue whispered, the words almost choking her. "Did you know?"

"News to me," Julia lied, her cheeks darkening. "She's just a normal woman, Sue."

"There's nothing *normal* about her," Sue whispered, her eyes wide as she drifted towards the sitting room. "She's a *star*!"

"She's a *diva*," Hilary interjected bitterly. "She makes Katie look like a little angel."

When they walked into the sitting room, Katie bounced up off the antique couch, a grin spreading across her gloss-covered lips. Despite only having given birth three months previously, she was back in her low-cut tops, her peroxide hair was curled wildly away from her head, and her skin was covered in an inch of dense makeup. Her appearance might have reverted back to normal, but she was now a kinder and warmer woman beneath it.

Katie had pushed the furniture out of the way and had laid out three baby mats with mobiles above them, which she had surrounded with overflowing baskets of toys. Baby Vinnie lay in the middle of the mess, blinking up at the ceiling as he squirmed in a designer outfit.

"You're here!" Katie squealed, her voice as high-pitched as ever. "This was such a lovely idea, Julia! I've been dying to have someone for Vinnie to play with."

"How do you know Candy Bennett?" Sue blurted out, her eyes trained on Katie. "Are you friends?"

"Oh, we go way back," Katie giggled with a wave of her hand. "We both started glamour modelling for the same magazine. She went off into acting. I tried, but I could never remember my lines.

I haven't seen her in years, so it's been great catching up."

"You need to tell me *everything*," Sue said as she hurried towards Katie before pulling her back onto the couch. "I want to know *every* gritty detail."

As Julia unclipped Pearl and Dottie from their pram, she wondered if what Katie and Sue's relationship had needed all this time was a famous actress between them. After gently waking the twins with cuddles and kisses, Julia laid them on the play mats next to Vinnie. The babies did not look all that interested in each other, but it was nice seeing her brother with her nieces, even if Vinnie was technically the twins' uncle. She snapped half a dozen pictures on her phone while they kicked and squirmed as the mobiles twisted and jingled above them. Leaving them with Sue and Katie, who were gossiping like the best of friends, Julia ventured into the kitchen in search of the elusive actress.

Instead of finding Candy in her fur-trimmed dressing gown, Julia found Harold sitting at the kitchen island with a laptop. He glanced up at Julia and smiled meekly before returning to his screen. Even though she had not meant to talk with the quiet assistant, Julia ventured into the kitchen anyway. She wandered over to the double-doored

AGATHA FROST

refrigerator, which was covered in pictures from her father and Katie's recent holiday to the seaside. She grabbed a glass bottle of water from the fully stocked shelf before going in search of a bottle opener. She walked past Harold as he typed what looked like nonsense on his laptop screen. She rummaged through the drawers next to the sink until she found a tin opener with a bottle opener on the end. After cracking off the lid, she leaned against the sink sipping her water. She smiled in Harold's direction, and he smiled back, but his fingers did not stop typing.

"Has she got you working hard?" Julia asked, nodding at the laptop.

"I'm sorry?" Harold replied, his deep voice surprising her again. "Has who got me working hard?"

"Candy," Julia said. "You work for her, don't you?"

"No," he replied, his fingers suddenly stopping entirely as he narrowed his eyes on Julia. "I'm her husband."

Julia unintentionally choked on her water, her eyes darting away from Harold and down to the floor. Not only were Harold and Candy visually mismatched for husband and wife, but they had not given off any vibes that they were even friends, let alone spouses. The meeting she had witnessed in the dark alley the night of Shane's murder flashed through her mind, making her choke again.

"I'm sorry," Julia said, injecting as much lightness into her voice as she could muster. "I - I just - it's none of my business."

"You assumed because of the way she talks to me?" Harold replied flatly as he began slowly typing again. "You wouldn't be the first, and I doubt you'll be the last."

Julia watched him type, unsure of what to say. She thought back to the way Candy had clicked her fingers at him and how he had silently obeyed her. She was not one to judge other people's relationships, but she could not imagine treating Barker in such a way, nor could she imagine him bowing to her like a servant.

"I really am sorry," Julia offered. "Nobody wins when you jump to conclusions."

Harold stood up and walked over to the fridge. He looked as though he was going to grab a bottle of water, but his hand diverted to the beer. He walked across the kitchen and grabbed the bottle opener Julia had used before returning to his laptop.

"Between you and me, I feel more and more like

the staff as the days go on," he said as he fiddled with his glasses after taking a deep glug of the beer. "Especially since she decided she wanted to ship us out to the country to build this house. It's the last thing we needed right now, but when Candy gets an idea, nothing stops her."

Julia decided not to ask why it was the '*last thing*' they needed, despite wanting to know. She thought back to the conversation she had heard in the café yesterday and how Harold had urged Candy to compromise when it came to the finances. She should have known then it would have been out of turn for an assistant to make such a suggestion.

"Have you been married long?" Julia asked as she took the stool around the corner from Harold. "Must be strange to be married to someone that everyone knows."

"Let's just say when we married, she was still '*Candice*' and not '*Candy*'," Harold said with a forced laugh. "We met in college. I was studying scriptwriting, and she was studying acting. Our paths crossed long enough for us to fall in love. That was twenty years ago, though. How times have changed."

Julia noticed the sadness and anger in his voice. She had been in her own unhappy marriage for twelve years before moving back to Peridale and meeting Barker, so she knew how to spot the signs.

"So, you're a scriptwriter?" Julia prompted, nodding at the laptop. "I suppose that works out quite well with your wife being an actress. I bet you have a black book full of contacts between you."

Harold laughed coldly again before shaking his head. He took another deep glug of beer before spinning his laptop around.

"I write code," he said, tapping on the screen of nonsense. "Dull, but it's where the money is these days. The only time Candy's professional life crossed with mine is when I coded her website." Harold spun the laptop back around and sighed at the screen. "I tried to break into scriptwriting, but there are too many wannabe writers and not enough jobs for us all. I didn't make the cut. I had to come up with a backup plan, so I retrained after reading an article about how coding would be the '*next big industry*'. I got in before it became oversaturated, so I was one of the lucky ones. Now everyone and his grandmother can code, and don't even get me started about the outsourcing to India and Russia."

"Still, I bet websites are fun to make," Julia offered. "You get to be creative."

"Someone else designs them," he said. "I just

write the code to bring them to life. I mainly work on corporate stuff. I got to work on a game app last year, but that's the most fun I've had. I wouldn't be lying if I said it was soul-destroying work, but it keeps us afloat. The money is too good to pass up."

Julia picked up on how he had said, *'keeps us afloat'* instead of *'keeps me afloat'*. She thought back to the article she had read where Candy had insisted she was waiting for the right script to land in her lap, and then about the bridal magazine advertising a movie she had never heard of. It did not take a genius to add the pieces together.

"I do love her," Harold said suddenly, his kind eyes trained on Julia. "I really do. Under it all, she's still my Candice."

Julia smiled and nodded, wanting to believe Harold even though she did not trust that he believed his own words. She thought once again of the passionate exchange she had witnessed between Shane and Candy and immediately became uncomfortable in Harold's presence.

At that moment, Candy floated into the kitchen, her nose in the air, her eyes anywhere but on her husband. Harold sent a smile in her direction, but she headed straight for a cupboard where she grabbed a packet of kale crisps. On her way back to the door, she stopped in her tracks and turned to them, her eyes landing on Julia instead of Harold.

"You're the café lady?" Candy said with an extended slender finger. "I remember you."

Julia nodded, expecting Candy to offer to pay for the coffee she had abandoned on Friday. Instead, she merely shrugged, apparently pleased with herself for remembering the face of one of the '*little people*'. She glided out of the room and back upstairs, her appearance leaving behind an icy feeling in the air.

"I should get back to work," Harold said, his fingers already typing on the keyboard. "It was nice to talk to you -"

"Julia," she said quickly. "Julia South. It was nice to meet you properly, Harold."

Feeling upset on Harold's behalf, Julia hurried out of the room and back to the sitting room. She was about to tell Sue that she was leaving, but her sister was still deep in conversation with Katie, and the two seemed to be getting along. Her father, Brian, was playing with his son and granddaughters on the floor, so distracted that he did not notice Julia watching. It was an almost perfect scene, so Julia headed for the front door alone and made her way back to the village.

AS JULIA WALKED HOME, SHE REALISED HER decision to walk to the manor and soak up the good weather had been a bad one. By the time she reached the bottom of the lane leading up to her cottage, dark clouds had drifted in from the horizon, bringing light drizzle. Without an umbrella, Julia quickened her step and buried her hands deep in her coat pockets.

As she reached the building site, the clouds had fully opened, soaking her to the bone. She would have run all the way home if she had not seen a hooded figure standing in front of the gate. She slowed down, wondering who could be braving the rain to stare at the piles of rubble.

"Nasty weather," Julia called out as she approached the stranger.

When she spotted the tattooed hands pulling back the hood to reveal Alfie's face, she felt at ease. Something about the biker made her feel like she was around someone she knew well, even though she only knew his name.

"This place," Alfie called out into the rain as it lashed down around them. "This whole village feels wrong."

"Wrong?" Julia called back as she attempted to shield her eyes from the rain. "How?"

Alfie turned to her fully, his dark eyes filled with sadness. He thrust his hands into his pockets and looked up at the sky as though he was looking for an answer to give to her.

"I don't know," Alfie replied, the rain sticking his dark hair to his face. "Ever since I arrived, I've felt a bad vibe. I keep seeing someone."

"Who?"

"It doesn't matter," Alfie replied, his brows furrowed deep over his eyes. "I - I -"

"Who is it?" Julia cried. "Someone you know?"

"I - I don't know," Alfie replied. "It's ancient history now. I - I know it's not her - it *can't* be. It's just bringing everything back up."

"Bringing what back up?"

Alfie looked as though he was going to tell Julia everything that was on his mind, but a car sped up the lane, the bright headlights dazzling them both. As though the spell had been broken, Alfie blinked down at Julia, his frown deepening.

"I should go," Alfie cried. "I'm sorry."

Before Julia could ask anything else, the mysterious man hurried past her and back the way she had just walked. Standing in the rain outside Barker's old cottage, she watched the stranger disappear. She desperately wanted to chase after him to force his story out of him, but she knew it was not her place.

"Who are you, Alfie?" Julia whispered into the rain as it dribbled down her face. "Where have I met you before?"

Julia looked at the scene of the crime again, the pile of rubble calling to her. In the wind and the rain, she spotted something rustling exactly where Shane's body had been. She squinted into the rain, but her ageing eyesight failed her. She looked up and down the lane before slipping through the open gate, consoled by the fact the police had already released the land back to Candy to continue building.

Brushing her soaked hair out of her eyes, Julia crept towards the plastic object, its rustling beckoning her. In her mind's eye, she could see Shane lying face down in the stones. Pushing that away, she bent down and was surprised to see a sodden bouquet of a dozen roses beneath the crackling plastic. Julia spotted a soggy piece of card tucked between the flowers, a Pretty Petals logo jumping out at her. The handwritten note had leaked and bled, but Julia could still see the words clearly.

"'*I'm sorry*'," she read aloud. "'*I love you*'. Who left these?"

Julia put the card back in the flowers and looked back at the lane where Alfie had been standing moments ago. She straightened up, not liking where her mind was taking her. She almost wanted to take the roses back to her cottage to examine them carefully, but she had more respect than that. Someone had intentionally laid the bouquet where Shane had been, she just did not know who. Instead, she pulled her phone from her pocket and hastily snapped a blurry picture before the rain soaked her device.

After slipping through the open gate, Julia bolted up the lane, not stopping until she was leaning safely against the door in the warmth of her cottage. She stood there for a moment, catching her breath as the cold from her wet clothes set in. She kicked off her shoes, shrugged off her coat, and hobbled towards the bathroom where a hot bath was calling her.

"*Julia!*" Jessie cried from the sitting room, making her jump. "I've been trying to call you."

Julia looked into the sitting room where Jessie and Billy were sitting together on the couch, with Jessie's peculiar social worker, Kim Drinkwater, taking up the armchair near the roaring fire. Kim was too busy making her way through a box of chocolates to look up at Julia.

"You have?" Julia replied, checking her damp phone. "Oh, I put it on silent because the twins were asleep. *Kim*! What a pleasant surprise. I didn't realise we had a meeting today?"

Kim waved a hand as she stuffed another handful of chocolates into her mouth. Julia squinted at the box, recognising it as one of the boxes still left over from Christmas.

Kim, who had been Jessie's social worker since she had been a little girl, was a character if Julia had ever met one. Her eccentric and colourful choice in clothing and makeup coupled with her craving for sugar and clumsy nature meant it was always a strange experience when they held their meetings. Today, Kim was wearing a bright blue denim skirt, a pink wool jumper with a yellow cardigan over it, and bright blue clips keeping her hair out of her eyes. She had gold shadow all over her lids, and shiny pink gloss smeared across her lips and chin.

"Don't worry yourself," Kim exclaimed through a mouthful of chocolate. "It's not an official meeting. I was just in the area, so I thought I'd drop by. To tell you the truth, I had a date, but I don't think it'll work out. I tripped and spilt coffee all over his shirt. I don't think he was bothered about the stains, but the burns looked quite bad. Shame, really. He was quite handsome. Not as handsome as your Barker, but close enough."

Jessie cleared her throat and shot Julia a look that screamed '*get rid of her*'.

"Well, it's nice to see you," Julia said as she tucked her wet hair behind her ears. "Sorry about my state. I got caught in the rain."

"It's raining?" Kim asked casually as she selected her next chocolate. "These are *really* delicious. They look expensive. Hope you don't mind me eating them. Found them while Jessika was in the bathroom."

Julia bit her tongue, deciding it was probably best not to mention that they had been expensive; there were only three left.

"Finish them," Julia said, widening her smile. "It's my pleasure."

"Oh, you are too kind," Kim said as she plucked the final three from the box to throw them into her mouth in one go. She chewed them around for a moment, but that did not stop her from talking. "I have some news about the adoption."

"*Oh?*" Julia called out, hurrying to the back of the couch. "Good news?"

Jessie looked up at Julia, grabbing her hand. She

squeezed it as they watched Kim swallow the giant ball of chocolate. She licked her lips, checked that she had shovelled in every last piece, and glanced at her watch before standing up.

"I should get going," she said absently as she stared out of the window. "Oh, you're right. It *is* raining. I have another date in an hour. You can never be too proud to double book, not that you have that problem. I heard about Barker putting that lovely engagement ring on your finger. If you weren't so lovely, I'd hate you for it."

Kim let out a girlish cackle as she scooped up her heavy bag. Her purse, keys, and phone fell out. She quickly darted down to pick them up despite the tight nature of her skirt, which was entirely inappropriate for the weather.

"The adoption?" Julia pushed. "You have news?"

"Oh, yes," Kim said, tapping her chipped red nail-polished finger on her chin as though she had forgotten all about the reason she had even come to the cottage. "Everything should go through within the next couple of months. We've done all the checks and interviews, it's just a case of getting the paperwork sorted out."

"So, it's happening?" Jessie asked, an uncertain look on her face as she stared at Kim.

"Yes, Jessika," Kim chuckled as she roughly ruffled Jessie's hair as though she was a puppy. "I told you that you had nothing to worry about. You've come a long way, and you're settled. The adoption will be official before your eighteenth birthday."

Julia's heart swelled up in her chest. She was at a loss for words and suddenly wanted to offer Kim the other three boxes of chocolates she had left over from Christmas.

"That's excellent news," Julia said, her grin spreading from ear to ear as she stared down at Jessie, who had a similar look on her face. "The best."

"You'll make quite the family," Kim said, stubbing her foot on the coffee table as she passed it. "Where is Barker anyway? Do you want me to tell him the news myself?"

"He's in London," Julia said, almost relieved by the fact. "But I'll make sure to pass it on."

"Shame," Kim said with a sigh as she looked up and down the hallway. "I can smell his aftershave. It lingers."

With that, Kim headed to the door. As usual, she tripped over the threshold before hurrying down the path in the rain to her bright yellow Fiat

Cinquecento parked on the lane behind Julia's car. Julia closed the door behind her, the grin still plastered across her face. Jessie appeared in the hallway, her eyes wide like a deer caught in the headlights of a monster truck.

Without needing to say a word, they ran to each other, crashing together like long lost family meeting at the airport for the first time. Despite being wet, Jessie clung to Julia as though her life depended on it.

"It's happening," Jessie whispered into Julia's shoulder. "It's real."

Holding the back of Jessie's head, Julia looked over at Billy, who was standing awkwardly in the sitting room like a spare part. Julia's elevated mood quickly dropped when she noticed that Billy's t-shirt was on inside out as though he had put it on in a hurry.

"So, you were both here when Kim turned up?" Julia asked, trying to keep her voice light as she pulled away from Jessie. "Alone?"

"Yeah," Jessie said with a shrug. "What's for lunch?"

Jessie turned on her heels and walked into the kitchen, but Billy stayed glued to the spot in the sitting room, his cheeks bright red. Julia looked at his t-shirt again, and he suddenly seemed to realise what she had noticed.

"I should go," Billy said. "First day of work tomorrow. Don't want to be too tired."

Without saying goodbye to Jessie, Billy headed for the door. Julia walked into the kitchen, wondering if she should talk to Jessie about her suspicions of what they had been doing when Kim had turned up, but she decided it could wait. For now, they had good news to celebrate.

CHAPTER 6

"*'Teenage pregnancy'*?" Sue called over Julia's shoulder as she helped herself to a cake from the display cabinet. "Why are you searching for that on the internet? I hate to break it to you, sis, but you're a little past that." Sue cut herself a large slice of Victoria sponge cake before her eyes bulged. "Wait - you're not - *oh my* - are you?"

"*Pregnant*?" Julia cried with a shake of her head. "If I were, you'd be the first to know about it. I

99

think I caught Billy and Jessie up to something yesterday."

Leaning against the counter, Julia read through the article about how the rates of teenage pregnancy were at an all-time low since records began in the 1960s. Pictures of young mothers with prams littered the page, causing her fingers to shake as she scrolled through.

"You mean, you caught them - you know - doing *that*," Sue asked, suddenly abandoning her cake for the more interesting topic. "She must have been so embarrassed! Poor kid. I remember when Gran walked in on me kissing Martin Hapton when we were sixteen, and I thought I'd never live it down. I still see the disappointment in her eyes to this day."

"I didn't walk in on anything," Julia said. "Well, I think the social worker might have walked in on something, but by the time I got there, the only piece of evidence was that Billy's t-shirt was on inside out."

"Oh," Sue said, her teeth gritting and her mouth stretching out at the sides. "That sounds like they were -"

"*Don't!*" Julia cried, holding up her hand. "I've only just come to terms with Jessie being my daughter, and now I've got to wrap my head around all of this teenager stuff. It's like I'm raising a child in fast-forward."

"She's a smart girl," Sue offered as she took her cake to the table nearest the counter. "I don't think you're going to be a grandmother just yet."

"Accidents do happen," Julia said with a sigh as she scrolled to a picture of a girl who looked suspiciously like Jessie holding a pregnancy test. "Do I talk to her about it? I feel like I should, but I wouldn't know where to start."

"As the mother of two daughters, I have no idea," Sue mumbled through her first mouthful of cake. "Oh, Julia. You have a gift!" Sue swallowed and dabbed a napkin at her lips. "But we didn't have that. We didn't have a mum when we were that age, we had Gran telling us not to trust boys, and not to talk to strangers. I suppose it worked. Neither of us got into any sticky situations. Well, you married that awful man, but we pretend that didn't happen."

Julia thought back to being Jessie's age. She had been at college studying to be a baker and was working in a café not unlike her own on the weekends. Her only boyfriend up until that point had been a boy in high school, and the most they had done was hold hands. She had been too busy at seventeen to entertain the idea of dating, not that she would have known where to start. Jessie, however, seemed a lot more mature than Julia had been, and she had to give her credit for that.

"If they want to do it, they're going to do it," Sue said, stamping her finger down on the table. "They're young adults of legal age, so there's not much we can do to stop them. The best we can do is educate them, and make sure they're safe."

"Should I buy her some - I can't even say the word."

"*Condoms?*" Sue said, a grin tickling her lips. "If you want her to die of humiliation, then yes."

At that moment, Jessie's bike screeched to a halt outside, prompting Julia to slap the laptop shut. She wrapped her hands around the edge of it and pushed forward a smile she knew was too broad to look natural. Jessie walked into the café, her eyes instantly narrowing on Julia as though she could see through the plastic shell of the laptop to the article she had been reading.

"How were the deliveries?" Julia asked, beaming from ear to ear. "The weather held up."

"You're weird," Jessie said with an arched brow. "Why are you so weird?"

Sue smirked at Julia from behind her cake before

taking another bite. Julia widened her smile, unsure of what to say. A part of her wanted to blurt out the question and ask why Billy's shirt had been on inside out, but another part of her did not want to know.

"It's the murder," Julia said quickly, her cogs working overtime. "It's all I can think about at the moment."

Thankfully for Julia, the answer pacified Jessie, who merely shrugged and walked into the kitchen to collect her next lot of orders.

"I went to see Billy at the building site," Jessie called from the kitchen. "They're working him like a dog, but he seems to be enjoying it. I think he's just happy to be working."

"That's good," Julia said, her mind still on the article. "Did he say anything?"

"You mean, has he been spying for you?" Jessie asked as she pushed through the beads with another stack of boxes. "Everyone turned up for work, including that actress and her camp friend. Billy's been asking around about Shane, but nobody has anything nice to say about him. Homophobic, racist, generally mean. He sounds like a total -"

"*Roses!*" Julia cried, cutting Jessie off. "Did you see any roses at the building site?"

"Roses?" Jessie echoed, looking down her nose at

Julia. "Are you feeling alright? It's not the menopause, is it? I heard a woman talking about it on the bus, and she looked about your age."

From the sweat that was breaking out across Julia's forehead, she wondered if Jessie might have had a point. She quickly wiped it away with a napkin before laughing off the suggestion.

"Julia's still got at least a handful of good eggs in her," Sue announced. "My mother senses can smell them. They're bouncing around in there like pinball!"

"You're weird," Jessie said, staring at Julia before turning on Sue. "Both of you. Super weird."

Jessie shook her head and headed for the door. She stacked the boxes up in the basket before riding off, but not without giving Julia one final sceptical look.

"Really well played, big sis," Sue said with a wink. "I don't think she suspected a thing."

Flustered and embarrassed, Julia ran around the café wiping the already clean tables until she felt her cheeks cool down. Even though Jessie was a good kid, Julia was beginning to wish parenting teenagers came with a manual. As each day passed, Julia felt the landmines gathering around her; one misstep and it would all explode.

As Sue helped herself to a second large slice of cake, Dot hurried into the café wearing her '*Preserve Peridale's History*' t-shirt over the top of her stiff blouse, her silver brooch poking over the collar. She planted herself in Sue's seat before huffing dramatically. When neither Sue nor Julia asked what was wrong, she huffed again and slapped her handbag on the table.

"*Well?*" she cried. "Is nobody going to ask what's wrong?"

"What's wrong, Gran?" Julia and Sue chorused.

"Harriet's called the *whole* thing off!" Dot announced with a flourish of her hands. "She doesn't want to protest anymore. I was trying to rouse the girls for another go, but Harriet doesn't want to do it."

"A man has died, Gran," Julia reminded her as she got to work making Dot a pot of tea. "It's probably best to stay away for a while."

"Well, that's not the reason she gave me," Dot said with a heavy sigh as she pushed up her stiff curls at the back. "Said she was too busy with the flower shop. She wasn't too busy when she was running around the village recruiting people to join her little army."

"Do you even care about the development?" Sue

asked as she sat across from her gran after checking on the twins in their pram.

"Not in the slightest," Dot announced with a roll of her eyes. "But that's not the point, dear. I'm invested now, and I want to see it through, or at least cause a little trouble first. Nothing too outside of the law, but some hijinks never hurt anyone. But *no*! Harriet has slammed the brakes on, not that she seemed very committed after Candy embarrassed her at the demolition. It's probably why she didn't turn up to the meeting on the morning we found the body."

Something clicked in Julia's mind, making her head bolt up. She splashed hot water on her hand, making her wince.

"She never turned up at all?" Julia asked, her mind working overtime. "Did you ask why?"

"It never crossed my mind," Dot said with disinterest as she stared at Sue as she wrapped her lips around her cake. "I'll have a slice of whatever Sue is having, dear, and be quick with that tea. My mouth is so dry I could drink coffee, and you know how I feel about that."

Julia finished making the pot of tea and quickly plated up the final slice of the Victoria sponge cake with which she had not made a penny of profit thanks to her family's rumbling stomachs.

"Where did you say you were going after here?"

Julia asked Sue as she set the tray down on the table.

"Mulberry Lane," Sue replied after licking her lips for a final time. "In fact, I'm going to go now before the baby shop shuts. The boutique is usually too expensive for me, but they posted about a sale online, and you know I love a sale."

"I might tag along," Julia said, her eyes going blank as she vanished into her thoughts. "I think it's time I paid Harriet Barnes a little visit. Gran, do you mind watching the café for fifteen minutes?"

"Well, I was actually just about to go -"

"I'll be back before you know it," Julia said, diving in to kiss her gran on the top of the head. "Thank you. You're a star."

Before Dot could argue, Julia grabbed her coat and bag and left the café with Sue and the twins following right behind.

MULBERRY LANE WAS THE SHOPPING HUB of Peridale. It dated back to the 1700s, and aside from the modern displays in the windows, the street was relatively unchanged. The rooftops were sagging, the buildings were twisted, and the roads were still cobbled, but it had an unmistakable authentic charm. At the bottom of the winding street stood

Julia and Sue's father's antique barn, but that was not where they were going today.

"Are you going to interview her?" Sue asked giddily as they made their way to Pretty Petals. "Slip some truth serum into her tea to get her to confess to murdering that builder bloke."

"You watch too much TV," Julia replied, glad when she noticed Harriet behind the counter. "You should hurry to the baby shop before it shuts."

"But I wanted to eavesdrop," Sue begged. "See my wonderful big sister in action."

"I'm just going to ask her a few questions," Julia said as she pushed Sue further down the street. "I'll probably be out before you are."

Sue mumbled something under her breath as she reluctantly plodded across the cobbled road towards the baby boutique with the twins. Julia turned her attention to the display of crinkled roses in the window, which looked like an out-dated display from the previous week's Valentine's Day celebration. Had Harriet really been too busy with the protest to focus on her shop?

Julia pushed the door, the tiny bell signalling her arrival. Harriet glanced over her glasses, but she quickly looked back at the wreath she was crafting when she saw that it was Julia.

"I wondered when I'd be seeing you," Harriet mumbled through the pencil that was clamped in the side of her mouth. "I thought you would've come sooner."

"You did?" Julia replied as she weaved through the floral displays towards the counter. "Did Evelyn predict my visit?"

"Let's not play games, Julia," Harriet said as she plucked the pencil out of her mouth to scribble something in the open book on the counter. She slotted the pencil into the silver bun on the back of her head before resuming her work on the wreath. "If you've come to prod and poke me about the murder, you're wasting your time. I don't know anything, and I have two funerals, a wedding, and a Bar Mitzvah to prepare flowers for."

Julia watched as Harriet's fingers hastily worked, snipping the stems of flowers to create the '*DAD*' lettering on the wreath. She wondered if she should turn around and leave, but her questions had collected during the walk from the café.

"My reputation precedes me more than I'd like," Julia said jokingly. "I'm not here to accuse you of anything."

"But you're not here to buy flowers either, are you?" Harriet replied with a knowing smile. "Ask me what you want and make it quick. I have nothing to hide, and a list of orders to get through, and believe me, my clients are a lot scarier than you, Julia South."

Julia laughed, but it came out sounding awkward and stiff. She had always liked Harriet's forthrightness and ability to speak her mind but being on the receiving end was a different experience than admiring it from a distance. The phrase *'doth the lady protest too much?'* sprung to mind as Harriet's fingers continued to work. Deciding to stop beating around the bush, Julia pulled her phone out of her bag and retrieved the picture she had snapped at the building site. She squinted at the fuzzy image. Double tapping on the photo zoomed her in, but the roses were barely distinguishable from the rubble.

"Have you seen these before?" Julia asked, turning the phone around. "They're roses with a card from your shop that were left at the building site after Shane died."

"What am I looking at?" Harriet snapped as she peered over her glasses. "It looks like a burnt lasagne."

"It's a dozen roses," Julia said with a sigh as she pocketed her phone. "With a card from your shop, left on the exact spot where Shane's body was found. The card read '*I'm sorry. I love you*'."

Harriet peered over her spectacles at Julia, an amused smirk on her lips. She half-rolled her eyes before coughing and continuing on with her work.

"Is that all you've got?" Harriet chuckled with a shake of her head. "Look around you, Julia. It was Valentine's Day last week. Before you ask who bought a dozen roses recently, ask yourself how many bouquets of roses you think I might have sold this Valentine's Day. Twenty? Thirty? Last I checked, it was closer to fifty. And how many of those people do you think paid in cash, leaving no trace of who bought them? Heck, I'd even let you sift through the card orders if you really wanted to, even though we both know that's against the data protection laws, but be my guest. And last time I checked, it wasn't illegal to leave flowers at the site where somebody died. In fact, it's very common and polite to do so, but I suppose in your narrowed sleuthing vision, everything is a clue, right?"

Julia's head recoiled into her neck, her eyes wide as she soaked in the barrage of words Harriet had just laid on her. If she was a more prideful woman, she might have bitten back, but as it were, she listened to the logical voice in her mind. She inhaled deeply, soaked in what Harriet had just said, and smiled.

"You're right," Julia replied. "You're absolutely right about every single thing you just said."

"Then are you done?" Harriet asked, plucking her pencil from her hair again to scribble something else in her book. "Because you've already got me behind."

Julia scrambled through her questions, most of which had revolved around trying to suss out who had left the flowers. She remembered what her gran had said and felt a renewed sense of control over her thoughts.

"I heard you arranged a protest meeting for the morning Shane's body was discovered," Julia began. "I happened to be there, and you didn't show up."

"I was sick."

"You seem fine now."

"It was one of those twenty-four-hour things."

"So, when did you arrange the meeting?" Julia asked, narrowing her eyes on Harriet. "That morning? The night before? What time exactly?"

"Around four in the afternoon the day before," Harriet replied, her hands stopping for the first time since Julia arrived. "Why does that matter?"

"Oh, I'm sure it doesn't," Julia said airily. "It's

just, by my estimations, and I'm sure the autopsy will reveal something similar, I think Shane died between six that night and seven the next morning. Where were you between those times?"

"At home," Harriet answered quickly without a second thought. "Like I said, I was sick."

"For twenty-four hours," Julia replied with a nod. "I see. And were you home alone?"

"I was with my cat," Harriet said, crossing her arms over her chest. "I didn't leave my cottage all night, and I went to bed around eight. Like I said, I wasn't feeling well. The reason I didn't turn up to the meeting was because I didn't wake up. I took some medicine that knocked me right out, and when I did finally wake up around noon, it was because people kept phoning me about the murder."

Julia nodded and took in the information. They both knew it was the furthest thing from a concrete alibi. Without any other witnesses besides a cat, Harriet would not be able to prove that she was home or even feeling sick. Julia could push it, but she decided to change gears.

"And you've cancelled the protest because of the murder?" Julia pressed. "Or, that's what my gran said, at least."

"Well, yes," Harriet said with an uncertain nod.

"More or less. I didn't realise how much time I'd been putting into the petition, and I'd let my orders slip behind."

"So, you're happy to see the new building going up?"

"Of course I'm not!" Harriet cried. "But there's not a lot I can do about it now, is there?"

"And you thought you could do a lot on the morning of the demolition with the digger already there?"

Harriet's icy stare flickered for a moment as she tuned into the same frequency Julia was operating on. Her spine stiffened, and her lips tightened. She picked up a flower, aggressively snipped off the stem, and continued with her work.

"I really need to get on," Harriet said, her earlier arrogance evaporating. "I can't tell you any more than I already have. I'm telling you the truth, and if you don't believe me, I don't care. The police haven't visited me, so they obviously have nothing on me. You're barking up the wrong tree here, Julia, and you know it."

Julia knew that she might be, but Harriet had not managed to rule herself out. In fact, she had made Julia more suspicious than when she had first entered the shop. Considering what Harriet had just said, Julia turned and left the shop in time to meet up with Sue as she exited the boutique with handfuls of stuffed bags hanging off the pram's handles.

"I think I bought everything in their size!" Sue exclaimed enthusiastically. "She wasn't lying when she said it was a sale. Did you extract anything juicy from Harriet?"

"Time will tell," Julia said as she walked beside Sue back towards her café. "I'm not ruling anything out just yet."

CHAPTER 7

T he next day after closing the café and dropping another cake off at the B&B, Julia found herself taking a cancelled order of twenty cupcakes to the building site. When she arrived, the builders were enjoying a break after pouring the concrete foundations thanks to the dry weather. With Barker's cottage completely gone, the rubble cleared, and the outline of Candy's extravagant house in place, it looked like a different plot of land entirely.

Julia approached the builders, glad to see Billy and Alfie chatting to each other like old friends. When she approached, both of them looked nervous, but she guessed for different reasons.

"Leftover cupcakes from the café," she announced. "I thought you boys might appreciate them."

The builders cheered their thanks as she passed the box around, letting them take as many as they wanted. When they had finished, she left the box with Billy and walked across the building site to Candy and Mikey who were having a spirited conversation while staring at a broad blueprint. Their yellow hardhats and work boots clashed with their stylish clothes and model features, making them look like they were dressing up for an editorial photo shoot rather than a hard day of labour.

"It just looks so much smaller than we planned!" Candy cried, stabbing her finger on the plans. "You promised me it would look grand. I want opulence, not second best. It barely looks bigger than the rest of the houses around here. I don't want to blend in, Mikey."

"And you won't!" he assured her, a hand on her shoulder. "Babe, I promised you opulence, and that's what you're going to get. This house will say *'I own everything, including you'* to anyone who walks past. No one in - what's this village called? Peri Peri Chicken, or something?"

"Perinale," Candy said with a shrug. "I don't know. I should have really visited before I bought the plot, but it was so cheap, and I couldn't get away from rehearsals for the show. Trust me when I say the village looked a lot nicer in the pictures. And I didn't think the people would be so - *odd*. It's like something out of those horror stories you hear. I was looking online last night, and apparently, Perinale has had more murders than most places. I'm just waiting for the guy with a leather mask and chainsaw to turn up. No wonder it was so cheap."

"It's Peridale," Julia butted in as she carefully approached with a smile. "Peri-*dale*."

Mikey and Candy looked at each other, and then down at Julia with amused smiles. They towered over her, making her feel dumpy in her yellow vintage dress.

"You're the café lady," Mikey said. "I think I owe you some money for the coffee the other day."

"On me," Julia said, holding her hands up.

"Happens to the best of us."

"One gets so used to having things given for free that one forgets to pay," Candy said, the same dead smile from the magazine advertisement plastered across her plump lips. "I saw you at the manor yesterday. Are you a part-time cleaner?"

"Brian South is my father," Julia said. "And I suppose Katie is my step-mother, but we're the same age, so it doesn't really work out like that. And little Vinnie is my baby brother."

"Is that what the brat is called?" Candy asked through tight lips. "Kept me up all night screaming and crying."

"Babies do that," Julia said bluntly. "I heard you and Katie were friends back in her modelling days?"

Before Candy replied, Mikey rolled up the blueprint and headed over to the builders. He plucked a cupcake from the box before directing a speech at the team. Julia turned back to Candy, who was looking down at her like she was a beetle to be crushed under her boot.

"I've known Katie a long time," Candy said. "We were acquaintances and colleagues back then. It's merely a coincidence that I've ended up in the village she was from. I never actually expected her to come back here, but it's not like her career took off, is it? Still, we can't all have rich parents. Some of us need to work for our money. It's funny, as I look at you, I would have sworn you were older than Katie."

Instead of getting offended, Julia widened her smile. She found the compliment within the insult owing to the fact that she was natural, and Katie had a solid relationship with her dermatologist's needle.

"I was talking to your husband the other day," Julia said. "Nice man."

Candy narrowed her eyes and looked like she did not know whether to laugh or slap Julia. Instead, she did neither and smiled.

"Harold is - *Harold*," Candy said lightly. "Is there anything you wanted? This is private property, after all."

Julia wanted to blurt out what she had seen Candy doing with Shane in the alley, but she decided to keep that information to herself for now. Even though it would amuse Julia to see the look on Candy's face when she revealed that her secret affair was not so secret, she knew it would not serve her purpose.

"Did you have a nice Valentine's Day?" Julia asked casually as she glanced over at the builders as they got back to work. "Do anything romantic?"

"I was at the manor," Candy said quickly.

"Working through plans. Why do you want to know?"

"No reason," Julia said with a shrug. "Just making conversation since we're going to be neighbours. So, you were in Peridale before the demolition?"

"Mikey and I came early to get a feel for the plot before we finalised the plans. I kept my head down though. I didn't want a media circus turning up. Plus, I needed to sweet talk the council to hurry them up with their planning permission. Didn't take too much work because I am incredibly famous."

"Indeed," Julia replied through almost gritted teeth. "I just assumed you'd arrived on the day you came into my café asking for directions."

"We'd been for a walk and couldn't get our bearings," Candy said curtly before turning her attention to the builders. "You ask a lot of questions for a café worker. Are you a reporter, or something? If this conversation turns up on a blog, I will sue you."

"I'm just a simple local business owner," Julia said with a sweet smile. "And your closest neighbour. I'm sure we'll have much to talk about over the coming months."

Candy looked disgusted by the idea, but she

plastered on her fake smile once again. Before Julia could ask any more questions, Candy hurried past her, stepping hard into a puddle next to Julia and splashing wet mud up her leg.

As Julia wiped it off with a tissue from her bag, she watched Candy and Mikey talk. From the way they kept looking over at her, she knew what their topic of conversation was.

Knowing that Candy had been in the village over Valentine's, Julia wondered if she had been the buyer or recipient of the flowers, and if so, what had she been apologising for on the card?

"You look deep in thought there," Alfie said, suddenly appearing above her. "Anything interesting?"

Julia scrunched up the muddy tissue and tossed it into the yellow skip nearby. Straightening up, she dusted down her skirt, turning her attention to the tattooed stranger. As Alfie smiled at her, his dark eyes dazzling, the feeling of comfort and familiarity washed over her again.

"Nothing important," Julia said, pushing Candy to the back of her mind for now. "How were the cupcakes?"

"Delicious," Alfie replied as he stuffed his hands deep into his pockets. "That's why I came over actually. I wanted to tell you how enjoyable they were. I haven't had cupcakes that nice since I was in Paris."

"You've been to Paris?" Julia echoed. "I've always wanted to go. What's it like?"

"As beautiful as you think it's going to be," Alfie said with a dreamy smile as he slipped into his memories. "If there weren't as many tourists, you could get lost in the romanticism. Most big cities in Europe are like that. Their culture and history make you want to be able to wander their streets alone for as long as you need so you can soak up every ounce of what they have to offer."

"You sound like you've travelled a lot."

"I spent most of my teens and early twenties bouncing from country to country," he said, pulling up the sleeves of his high-visibility jacket. "It's where I got these. Every time I visited somewhere new, I got inked. Ended up in my fair share of hospitals with nasty infections from unskilled artists, but it only made me appreciate our national health even more. You don't realise how lucky you are until you've been sat in a boiling waiting room for seven hours in the middle of New Delhi with a green arm."

"I bet you're a funny man to have a drink with,"

Julia said. "The stories would never stop."

"I've heard that before," Alfie said with a nod. "I probably owe you a drink as an apology for the other day when you caught me in the rain. I was too lost in my thoughts to act like a polite human being. I'm sorry for running off."

"Don't mention it," Julia said, holding up her hands. "If you catch me in The Plough before you leave, I'll let you buy me that drink, but you don't have to apologise. You seemed to have a lot on your mind."

"You don't even know the half of it," Alfie said with a strained laugh. "It's been a crazy week."

Julia thought back to the naked meeting with Shane at the top of the stairs, and she suddenly itched to know the reason behind it. She looked into Alfie's eyes, and she felt he knew exactly what she was thinking. Had the cause of the altercation been enough for Alfie to resort to murder? Julia could feel her heart tugging her away from that thought, but her logical brain knew it was a possibility.

"Did you find your girl?" Julia asked, eager to move the conversation along. "You said you kept seeing someone?"

"I did?" Alfie mumbled, almost to himself as his cheeks darkened. "It's honestly nothing. I was having a bad day. I let some old stuff get the better of me."

"It happens to the best of us," Julia offered with a shrug. "But if you ever need someone to talk to, I have a café where there are more cupcakes where those came from, and I've been told I'm a good listener."

"I really appreciate that," Alfie said with a smile so genuine, Julia was not sure he could be capable of murdering someone. "You're cool, cake lady."

"Someone else has called me that," Julia chuckled as she thought of Jessie. "Maybe I should change my name?"

"Maybe," Alfie said with a nod as he stepped back. "I might take you up on that offer of more cupcakes. I need to get back to work, but thanks for being so cool. I've met a lot of people on my travels, but not everyone is so kind."

Alfie flashed her one last smile before turning on his heels and hurrying back to the builders. He ruffled his dark hair and got to work smoothing out the concrete.

As Julia headed to the gate, a pink Range Rover pulled up outside, and Katie's window wound down. She waved to Candy, who waved back before passing her hardhat to Mikey. She ran to the gate, pushing

Julia out of the way. Before she climbed into the car, she kicked off her boots and pulled a pair of heels out of her large handbag.

"There's a retail park out of town that's open until ten," Julia heard Katie say as she wound up the window.

Julia watched the pink Range Rover zigzag its way down the lane. If Candy was upset about Shane's death, she really was a great actress after all. Julia knew she would have to confront her soon if only to see her reaction as she dug beneath the perfect exterior, but she would wait for the right time.

"Wait up!" Billy called to Julia as she unclipped the gate. "They've let me finish early because there's not a lot I can do. I told Jessie I'd meet her after work, so I'll walk up with you."

"Sounds good to me," Julia said, looking past Billy to Mikey, who was sitting on an upturned crate with his face in his hands and the blueprint cast on the floor. Without his actress employer glued to his side, Julia suspected Mikey was a slightly different person from the one she had seen so far. Turning away from him, Julia turned to Billy and smiled. "There's something I need to talk to you about anyway."

Billy gulped and nodded, and it was obvious he knew exactly what Julia was thinking about. They set off in silence, neither of them saying anything until they turned the bend and the building site was out of view.

"I know you probably think you're more grown up than you are," Julia said as she reached into her handbag, "but the worrying is keeping me awake at night, so I'm giving you these because I need to know you're being safe."

Julia pulled out the box of condoms Sue had bought for her. She pushed them into Billy's hands, but he stared down at them with such a look of horror that Julia immediately regretted her decision to intervene.

"Miss S, we don't need these," Billy said, the bravado gone and his voice that of a little boy. "We were -"

"If you're already being safe, that's all I need to know," Julia said, her eyes trained on her cottage in the distance, the conversation making her feel uncomfortable. "I just want to know that Jessie's life isn't going to be derailed by something that can't be changed once it's done."

"Miss S," Billy started again, thrusting the box back to Julia, "we're not doing *that*. We're both waiting until we're ready."

"But I saw -"

"My inside out t-shirt?" Billy jumped in. "Yeah, we were kissing. Ya'know, the usual stuff. Jessie spilt her cola on me, so we put my shirt in the tumble dryer to dry it off. Kim came in, so I quickly grabbed it and put it on. I didn't realise it was inside out until I saw you staring at it. Swear down, Miss S, I love Jessie too much to pressure her into that stuff."

Julia stopped in her tracks to stare down at Billy. He looked scared of her, and she wondered if this was what Candy had wanted when she had stared down at Julia. Billy gulped, but he appeared to be telling the truth.

"Maybe I've jumped to conclusions," Julia said as she continued walking. "But I still want you to have these."

She thrust the box back to Billy and then put her hands in the pockets of her coat to stop him from passing them back.

"Miss S -"

"You're both smart kids," Julia said loudly as they reached the cottage. "And eventually, if you stay together, the time will feel right, and that's natural. I don't want to be one of those parents who can't be talked to about these things because that's when problems happen. Keep them in your drawer and ignore them until you think you need them. Okay?"

Billy nodded as he quickly stuffed them into his pocket. Julia pushed open her gate, her face bright red. She felt as though she had just wrestled a lion that had turned out to be a bunny in a costume.

"Not a word of this to Jessie," Julia whispered to Billy as she pushed on the door. "Do you understand?"

Billy nodded as he bent down to kick his muddy boots off before entering. Julia stepped into her cottage, the scent of beef instantly hitting her. She waited for Billy to come in before closing the door behind him. She planted a hand on his shoulder and gave him a reassuring smile before nodding for him to go and find Jessie.

"Hi, honey, I'm home!" a voice cried from the kitchen. "Did you miss me?"

Barker appeared in the doorway, once again wearing Julia's frilly apron. His beaming smile was just what Julia needed to see.

"I thought you were getting the last train back?" Julia asked as she hurried forward to hug him. "I was going to bake you your favourite cake."

"I rearranged the last meeting to could get an

earlier train to surprise you," Barker said after kissing her. "I'm cooking - *well* - I'm attempting to follow a recipe. I don't know how it's going, but how hard can cottage pie be to make? Jessie chopped the vegetables for me."

Julia inhaled Barker's aftershave, glad to have him back home. With the murder swirling around in her mind while sleeping in an empty, cold bed, the nights had dragged on without him.

"How were the meetings?" Julia asked as she followed Barker into the kitchen where a bottle of white wine and two glasses were waiting for them. "Get lots ironed out?"

"Like you wouldn't believe!" Barker exclaimed as she walked over to the bubbling mince mixture in the pan on the stove. "I think they really believe in this book. They were talking about magazine interviews and daytime TV slots. I don't know if it's all fluff talk to get me excited, but they're making all the right noises. They gave me some sales estimates today, and they think we can shift enough to crack the top one hundred chart, but I'm not holding my breath."

"It is a good book, Barker," Julia reminded him. "Better than I expected."

"I'll take that as the compliment I think you

intended it to be," Barker said with a smile over his shoulder as he stirred the mixture, slopping some over the edge and onto the hob. "They've given me a list of things that I need to sort out myself. They want me to set up a website to start a blog. I have no idea where to start with that. Do you think Jessie will know?"

"I know a guy," Julia said, sitting upright. "Candy's husband, Harold, makes websites. It's his job."

"Candy Bennett?" Barker replied with an arched brow. "I didn't even know she was married."

"Neither did I, but trust me when I say he's nothing like her. He's actually really nice. He's staying at the manor, so I think he'll give you a discount considering the man he's staying with is soon going to be your father-in-law."

"Does that mean Katie will be my mother-in-law?" Barker asked with a laugh. "She's younger than I am!"

The notion had not crossed Julia's mind before, but she giggled at the thought of having to explain that situation to strangers. Jessie walked in, a small black box in her hands and a sheepish look on her face.

"We're going out," Jessie said as she looked

down at the box. "Give you two some alone time. Billy wants to take me to the cinema. There's a superhero film about some panther dude that everyone is raving about. I suppose this is what it's like to be a normal teenager."

"You've come a long way from that girl living on the streets," Julia said, stroking her cheek with a finger. "What's in the box?"

Jessie looked down at it and pulled it away from Julia for a moment before holding it out with shaky hands. Julia accepted it, unravelled the black ribbon, and snapped it open. She stared down at a silver locket, '*Julia and Jessika*' engraved on the surface.

"It's a year today that you caught me stealing cakes from your café," Jessie said, her cheeks instantly blushing. "A year exactly since you took a chance on me when no one else would and changed my life."

Welling up, Julia pulled the locket from the box, her fingers shaking more than Jessie's. She fiddled with the clasp before unlocking it, a picture of Julia on one side, and one of Jessie on the other.

"It's beautiful," Julia whispered, clenching the locket in her hand. "I didn't even realise."

"It's just a date," Jessie said with a shrug. "But I'll never forget it as long as I live."

Julia reached out and yanked Jessie into a hug. She cried happy tears into Jessie's hoody, unable to stop them from flowing.

"I love you," Julia whispered. "And I'm so proud of you."

"Yeah, I love you too," Jessie replied as she pried Julia off her. "But don't make it weird. The film starts soon, so I need to go."

Jessie gave her one last smile before hurrying down the hallway towards Billy. When the door slammed behind them, Julia unclasped her fist and looked down at the locket again. She could not believe it had been an entire year since she had caught a scared little girl with a dirty face and ratted hair stealing cakes from her café because she was starving and liked Julia's baking. In that time, she had watched Jessie grow from a little girl into a young woman, and she meant it when she said she was proud.

Barker took the locket from Julia and looked down at it, also seeming on the verge of tears. He brushed Julia's hair out of the way and clipped the chain around her neck. The locket fell and landed just next to her heart. She rested a hand on it, vowing to wear it until the day she died.

"You've raised a good kid there," Barker

whispered as he cupped Julia's face in his wide palm. "You should be proud."

"She'll be *our* kid soon," Julia replied, her lips trembling. "You weren't here, and I didn't want to tell you over the phone. Your favourite social worker visited with good news. The adoption has been approved. We're going to legally be her parents before she turns eighteen in May."

Barker pulled Julia into his chest, and even though she knew he was trying to hide it, she felt a teardrop drip onto her ear. The mince mixture bubbled over the side and fizzed against the gas flames, but it did not matter. Exactly one year ago, Julia had woken up on this day with a looming divorce and an unclear future, but one year later, she had so much to live for.

CHAPTER 8

J ulia became increasingly restless as the days passed and no new information surrounding Shane's murder surfaced. A piece in *The Peridale Post* told of his simple, working-class upbringing in the northern town of Burnley. He had a divorce under his belt, but the union created no children. His parents were dead, and the only insight into his personal life revolved around his work as a builder.

With so little to go on, Julia had pushed Barker into calling DS Christie to find out more information, but there was nothing to tell. Forensics had not found anything of note at the scene and could only confirm that the bloody brick located at the scene was the murder weapon. The autopsy had uncovered that he had eaten a burger not long before his death and that his approximate time of death was somewhere between midnight and four in the morning.

When Sunday rolled around again, Julia convinced Barker to visit Peridale Manor to talk with Harold about building a website. Julia did not care if Harold could do the job, but she did want to talk to him again. Harold's name sat last on her list of suspects, behind Candy, Harriet, and Alfie, but he was the only one with a large question mark next to his name.

"It's happening so fast," Barker said as they passed the building site. "I overheard the architect say he's had all the pieces built off-site to get it finished quicker."

Julia slowed down and looked at the tall, metal structure that had popped up where Barker's cottage had once stood. She had only realised the sheer scale of the project when the framework had been erected, and she could not help but feel that Harriet had a point after all. It looked unlike anything else in Peridale, lacking any of the village's charm or personality. Julia liked to think she was comfortable with progress, especially after spending so many of her adult years living in a big city, but the building made her feel defensive of the village she adored.

"Candy would have built that same house wherever she bought her land," Julia said as she sped up and continued down the tight lane. "She doesn't care about Peridale one bit."

They soon arrived at the manor, and Candy's black Range Rover let Julia know the actress was home, but she had no interest in speaking with her anytime soon. She was still her prime suspect, but she knew very little was to be gained from talking to the egotistical woman. If she were to uncover Candy as the culprit, it would have to be through other means.

Hilary let them in and showed them to the study, where Harold had set up a temporary office.

"Just one second," Harold said, barely looking up as his fingers continued to type. "Let me just finish this last line of code and then I - *done*! Oh, hello again. It's Julie, right?"

"Juli-*a*," she corrected him with a polite smile.

"Don't worry. It happens more than you'd think. I hope we're not interrupting anything."

"Not at all," Harold said, offering them the two seats in front of the large mahogany desk, which sat in the middle of the dark, book-lined room. "I'm only working on an app update today. I'm ahead of schedule as it is so I can take a break."

Julia and Barker took the two seats. It was unusual for Julia to see someone else behind the desk that her father usually occupied when he was making phone calls and sending emails while buying and selling antiques. Unlike her father, Harold did not quite suit the grand room around him. He was wearing a printed t-shirt, which was a little too tight around the stomach and arms, and a pair of fabric shorts that would have been more suited to a skateboarding teenager than a middle-aged coder.

"'*Empire Strikes Back*'," Barker said with a grin as he nodded at Harold's t-shirt. "Still one of the best films of all time."

"You're not wrong there, my friend," Harold replied, his grin matching Barker's. "Cinematic perfection that has yet to be matched. What would our childhoods have been without those films?"

"Dull," Barker replied. "I'm Barker Brown, Julia's fiancé. I heard you build websites? I might be in the market for one."

"Oh?" Harold said, leaning against the desk after half-closing his laptop. "What sector are you in, my friend?"

"I'm an author," Barker said somewhat nervously. "Well, soon-to-be-published author through *Mystery Triangle Publishing*. My publicist wants me to set up a website to start blogging. I don't really understand it, but he made it sound important."

"I've heard of those guys." Harold nodded, seeming a little impressed. "You must be good. So, you're looking for a simple website where you can write blogs for social sharing?"

"Those are the exact words my publicist used!" Barker cried, pointing at Harold. "*Social sharing*! I don't even know what that means. If I'm totally honest with you, I don't trust any of it. The kids these days share far too much online."

"You're too young to be talking like that, my friend," Harold said with a deep chuckle. "I can sort you out. In fact, if you've got an hour, I can get you something set up today, and I'll even show you the basics."

"How much will all that cost?" Barker asked. "They said they'd cover the costs, but on a thirty-day invoice."

"Let's say one hundred to you," Harold said with a shrug. "Setting up profiles is easy. I have some other sites that I've built that are similar. I'll just change up some of the colours. Once I've taught you how to use it, you'll be set."

Barker moved his chair around the desk so that he was next to Harold, leaving Julia to mull over her thoughts. Instead of watching them, she walked around the room and glanced over the spines of the thick leather-bound hardbacks that lined the walls. Instead of thinking about the books, she was thinking about the questions running through her mind. If Harold had killed Shane, his only motive would have been the affair between Candy and Shane. If Harold did not know about the affair, he had no reason, therefore ruling him out of the picture entirely. As Julia listened to Barker and Harold discuss the more delicate details of the blog, she tried to think of a way to uncover information without asking the man outright.

"The house is coming along nicely," Julia said, turning towards the desk with a book open in her hands when there was a break in conversation. "It certainly looks big."

"Don't let Candy hear you saying that," Harold

whispered, his eyes flashing a hint of bitterness. "She thinks Mikey has tricked her and not designed the house to scale. She wanted something as big as this manor, not that we had the budget for it."

"I'm sure it'll look fine when it's finished," Julia offered as she slammed the dusty book shut. "I bet you're both glad work has resumed after that dreadful incident with - Oh, what was he called? The builder who was in charge? My memory is like a sieve."

Julia clicked her fingers as though trying to conjure up the name. She shot Barker a look that she hoped said '*be quiet*' when she noticed his lips forming the letter *S*.

"Shane?" Harold offered after a long pause.

"That's it!" Julia exclaimed, snapping her fingers with a flourish. "Shame about what happened to him. Did you know him?"

"Not really," Harold replied without looking up from the laptop screen. "He came across as a bit of a pig. Overheard him saying some stuff to Candy about Mikey being '*queer*'. My brother's gay, so I didn't like that. We're living in a different time now, so it's shocking that people like that still exist. Well, not that he exists anymore, but people *like* him do."

Julia thought back to hearing that same word

leave Shane's lips when he had been standing naked on the landing after throttling Alfie. The word had made her feel uncomfortable then, but it made her feel even more uncomfortable to know that it had not been a one-off.

"So, you'd say you didn't like him?" Julia pushed as she carefully put the book back on the shelf. "I suppose you only had a couple of days to get to know him?"

"Shane arrived when we did," Harold corrected her as he continued to type. "Just before Valentine's Day. Mikey wanted him here because he'd be leading the project, although look how that turned out."

Julia soaked up the information, but she did not say another word. She had wondered how long Candy and Shane's affair had been going on, but she would not be surprised if it had started during that week before the build began. Had Harold discovered what they were doing, or had he been oblivious to his cold wife's infidelity? Julia thought about how she had seen them in the alley, and how they had not been cautious about not being seen.

"Did Candy like him?" Julia asked, knowing that the question was one too far when she heard it leaving her lips.

Harold stopped typing for a moment, his eyes darting up at Julia. They lingered for a second, everything she needed to know in his weary gaze. He gulped hard before looking back down at the screen with tense brows.

"I really need to concentrate on this," Harold muttered, his typing twice as fast as before. "I can only afford to work on this for an hour."

Despite his earlier admission that he was ahead of schedule and that the work for Barker would be easy, Julia stayed quiet.

"Why don't I get you both some coffee?" Julia offered, her tone sweet. "And I'll see if there are some biscuits too."

Julia slipped out of the room with a smile. When she closed the door behind her, she leaned her head against the wood and let out a deep breath. Opening her eyes, she saw Hilary wiping the counter in the kitchen while shaking her head at Julia. Julia smiled back, but the elderly housekeeper tutted and hobbled off with her stick. Julia could almost hear Hilary saying '*that woman is always up to something*' in her mind.

After making coffee and emptying half a packet of chocolate digestive biscuits onto a plate, Julia slipped back into the study. The men were hard at work, so she left them to it. She considered searching for her father or Katie, so she could spend time with her baby brother, but raised voices from the sitting room caught her attention.

Julia immediately recognised one of the voices as belonging to Candy. Keeping light on her feet, Julia crept as close to the archway leading into the sitting room as she dared. Standing next to a tall marble bust, she glanced inside. Candy and Mikey were sitting on opposite sofas, blueprints on the coffee table between them. Neither of them looked happy with the other one, and Mikey seemed on the verge of tears.

"You signed off on this months ago!" Mikey said, his high-pitched voice shallow and small. "I promise I haven't changed a thing since then."

"Then you've done something wrong!" Candy screeched, her voice piercing. "Because what I saw this morning was *not* the house I wanted. It's *tiny*! Did you use a toy ruler to measure things out?"

"It's the *exact* same!" Mikey cried, followed by the rustling of paper. "I promise you, Candy. This is what you wanted. It's going to look a little funny until the walls are installed. I put all of these windows in because you wanted the house to feel spacious. Look at this one right at the front. It's floor to ceiling over two floors. It's going to feel huge inside!"

"I don't want it to *feel* huge," she yelled back. "I want it to *be* huge. Sort this out, Mikey, or your reputation in this business will be ruined. Don't forget who I am or the power I have."

Julia heard the rip of paper, followed by clicking heels on floorboards. She pressed herself against the wall and ducked behind the bust as Candy burst out of the sitting room. She walked right past Julia, but she did not notice her. After grabbing a bundle of keys from the table next to the door, she headed outside. There was a crunch of gravel followed by the screeching of tyres as she sped down the lane in her giant car. Julia turned back to the sitting room as faint sobs echoed around the grand space. Without a second thought, Julia crept into view and approached Mikey as he picked up the two halves of his ruined blueprint.

"It's a good job I make copies," Mikey laughed through his tears as he quickly wiped them away when he saw Julia. "Nothing lost."

"Are you alright?" Julia asked softly, unsure if she should approach. "I just saw Candy storm out."

"That's just Candy," he said, laughing through his tears.

Julia thought that was all she was going to get, but Mikey fell back into the sofa, his eyes trained on her as he lifted the back of his hand up to his mouth. He shook his head before the tears started to silently fall down his face. Julia hurried forward and sat next to him to wrap her arm around his narrow shoulders. Mikey melted into her like a boy desperate for his mother. The sobbing grew and grew until it came to an abrupt stop.

"Look at me," Mikey muttered as he wiped tears from his streaked cheeks. "I'm so embarrassed. Look what she's reduced me to."

Mikey wiped his damp hands on his skin-tight jeans before running them over his platinum blond buzz cut. He inhaled deeply, before pushing forward a smile and turning to Julia.

"Please tell me this village has a bar," he asked. "I'm in desperate need of a drink."

"I know a place," Julia said as she nodded to the door. "C'mon. I could use one myself."

CHAPTER 9

Mikey looked less than impressed when he had to climb into Julia's vintage aqua blue Ford Anglia, and even less impressed when they pulled up outside The Plough.

"It's not a bar, but it's the best Peridale has to offer," Julia said apologetically as she pulled her keys from the ignition. "And it's cheap."

"Well, Lord knows I need to save money right now," Mikey said as he grabbed the door handle.

"I'm ruined if Candy fires me this far into the project."

Sundays were usually spent only a couple of ways in Peridale. There were the people who spent their mornings at St. Peter's Church, and then the people who spent their mornings at the pub. Julia fell into neither category, instead usually choosing to sleep in or run errands, but on this morning, she was glad to be at the pub with Mikey.

Despite the chilly weather, the tables in front of the pub were filled with the smoking residents of Peridale. Inside was just as packed, with the chairs and tables closest to the fireplace the most filled. After ordering their drinks, both of them opting for dry white wine, they found a table in the corner.

"You weren't wrong about it being cheap," Mikey said as he stared into the wine. "You get so used to city prices, you forget how little things cost in the sticks. No offence."

"None taken," Julia said as she took her seat. "It's not bad wine either."

Mikey sat across from Julia, his back to the rest of the pub. His unusual buzz cut, bright clothes, and feminine manner garnered a few raised eyebrows, but most did not look up from their pints. After taking his first sip of wine, Mikey seemed to calm down a little, although there was still a shake to his hands.

"What's your story?" Julia asked him, her finger circling her glass as she stared into the flickering flames of the fire. "How did you end up here?"

"In Peridale?" he asked, arching a perfectly defined brow that she was sure had been aided with a pencil. "I designed the house."

"I meant '*here*' in the general sense," she corrected herself. "Here in life. Are you happy?"

"Is anyone?" he scoffed before taking a deep gulp of wine as though it were water. "I bounce from job to job designing houses for rich people, I get to keep a fraction of the cost, and then I scurry back to wherever I came from until the next job comes along."

Mikey looked as though he was going to cry again, but another sip of wine steadied him. Julia decided against diving into her drink just yet. She knew she had a chance to find out more about Candy from someone who might be in an excellent position to tell her things off the beaten track.

"Where is home?"

"Today, it's Peridale," he announced. "When this job is finished, I've got a month left on my flat in London, but between you and me, I can't afford it. I try to keep up with the lifestyle, but it barely keeps up with me. Maybe I'll go up north. I hear property costs nothing up there."

"But where is home?" Julia repeated. "Where are you really from?"

Mikey looked down at a silver band on his wedding finger that Julia had not noticed until now. He fiddled with it a little, but he did not let his attention linger.

"I haven't worn this for two years," he explained when he noticed her eyeing up the ring. "Let me see yours?" Julia held out her hand, and Mikey assessed the pearl. "It's beautiful. I hope he loves you."

"Thank you," she said, hearing the sadness in his voice. "It was my mother's engagement ring first. And he does love me, and I love him."

Julia's admission of being in love looked like it might push Mikey back to the verge of tears. He drank more of his wine, taking it past the halfway point. A little hiccough told her he was not used to drinking so fast.

"Hold on tight," Mikey said, looking down at his ring again with a sad smile. "I thought I'd found him. *The one.* Do you know how hard it is to date as a gay man? You crawl the bars and the apps, jumping from bed to bed, trying to find something that resembles happiness. You find it in fleeting moments, but they get bored and move onto the next thing. I met Kirk in a bar. I'd been stood up on a date, and he bumped into me. I threw my drink at someone else in anger thinking it was them. They kicked me out of the bar. Kirk came after me, laughing at the top of his lungs. He told me he'd bumped into me, by accident, of course. I wanted to hit him for getting me thrown out, but there was something in his smile. It was addictive. I started laughing too, and I knew I'd found the man I wanted to marry. And we did. Six months later, we tied the knot. Oh, I poured everything into it. My time, my money, my energy. Candy was there too. We'd just finished an apartment project together. She wanted to redesign her London pad to sell it. We made a tidy profit, but my cut went into the divorce six months later."

Mikey paused, his voice vanishing. He gulped hard, not looking like he could go on. Julia reached under the table and gave his knee a reassuring rub.

"Kirk came to me and told me he'd found someone else," Mikey continued, his voice strained. "Said he'd found '*the one*'. I told him he was my '*the one*', but he said I wasn't his. He said we'd rushed into it, and that it was silly. The sad thing is, I knew he was right. I had clung so hard to that glimmer of happiness that I tried to force it into reality. I wanted to believe I could be the one. I wanted to believe it was *my* turn for the fairy tale. I wanted all the guys in those bars to see that I got out, and I'd made it. Our divorce finalised two years ago, and it took every penny I had. I've been living job to job, trying to maintain this image I built for myself. The apartments, the clothes, the hair, the look, and all for what? To impress some guy for a night whose name I won't remember in the morning?"

Mikey reached out for his glass with shaky hands, the ring more evident than ever. He finished the rest of the wine like it was his tonic to survive.

"Why are you still wearing the ring, Mikey?" Julia asked, her voice soft and calm. "I'm divorced. I know how it feels."

"To maintain the pantomime, of course," he cried, his lips wet with the alcohol. "Candy was at the wedding, but she wasn't at the divorce. We're not friends, we're business partners, and I don't even think we'll be that soon. She's been lashing out more than normal, and I'm not sure how much I can put up with it. I slipped the ring back on because I wanted to pretend to her that my life was brilliant and that I wasn't at rock bottom. I started to believe it, but when this is all over, I'll be back to having no one. I'm living out of a suitcase at the awful B&B next door, and I can *barely* afford that. If it wasn't for the deposit Candy gave me, I wouldn't have a penny."

Julia's heart broke for Mikey. It was one of the saddest stories she had ever heard, but she knew what he was going through. She had put off signing her divorce papers for months because she had not wanted to face the reality that she had failed at something, even though it had ended for good reasons. Since signing those papers, her life had gone from strength to strength, and she had found happiness again, not just in Barker and Jessie, but within herself. As she stared at Mikey, who was eyeing up her wine, she wondered how she could convey that to him. She thought about when she had been at her lowest and knew no words would make things better, so she slid the wine across the table.

At that moment, the builders from the B&B walked in, their roaring presence immediately felt by all. Julia and Alfie noticed each other at the same time, and they shared a smile. When Julia turned her attention back to Mikey, he was already well on his way to drinking Julia's wine.

"What is Candy like to work for?" Julia asked, eager to know more about the actress. "I sense she's not all she appears to be."

"You mean the lovely actress adored by all?" he scoffed loudly, sloshing the wine as he did. "Last time I checked, her career wasn't going so hot. She's a *fake*! A *fraud*! She doesn't have a nice bone in her body. She sniffs out happiness in people and snuffs it out because she's a witch. I hated working with her last time, but I didn't have a choice but to agree to build her house. If I'd have said no, I would have been risking it for another job that might not have come. It was either this, or the job centre, and could you imagine me working in a normal job?"

Julia smiled awkwardly as she watched Mikey cross the line from vulnerable to bitter. His entire face changed, each muscle twisting at the mention of Candy's name.

"You'll find someone one day," Julia assured him, unsure of what else to say. "And even if you don't, you'll always have yourself."

"I found someone," Mikey muttered as he stared into the wine. "Someone after Kirk, but nothing lasts, does it? I - I think I'm going to be sick."

Without another word, the slender architect sprinted across the pub and into the men's bathroom. Julia looked down at the wine, wondering if the alcohol or the conversation had turned his stomach. Either way, she decided she had not helped Mikey feel better in any way, and she had not learned much that she did not already know about Candy. She had suspected her public persona was nothing more than a front since their first meeting.

"Is he okay?" a soft voice asked, disrupting Julia from her thoughts. "He didn't look too good."

Julia smiled up at Alfie, who was hovering over the table with a pint in his hand. His dark hair was tucked behind his ears, and he was wearing a tight black t-shirt, which brought out the definition in his chest and stomach muscles. Earth-toned bracelets cluttered his wrists, a stark contrast against his tattooed skin. He had swapped his usually black nose ring for a gold one, and he was wearing gold studs in each ear. The feeling of familiarity washed over Julia again, but instead of making her feel comfortable, it made her shift in her seat.

"Can I ask you something?" Julia asked, squinting at the builder. "Have we met somewhere before? You look so - so familiar."

"A handful of times in the past week," he joked. "But before I came here? I don't think so. I get that a lot. I must have one of those faces. I think you'd remember if you'd seen a guy with all these tattoos."

Julia looked them up and down, the intricate designs all blending into one.

"You're right," she said with a nod, shaking her head. "It's just a feeling I can't seem to shake."

"Maybe in a past life?" he suggested with a knowing nod. "That is if you believe in those things. Evelyn has been educating me on '*the other side*'. It's all quite fascinating, but I'm not sure I'm sold yet. She gave me a tarot reading over breakfast and almost flipped the table when she turned over the cards. According to her, I have life-changing and important news coming my way today."

Mikey hurried out of the bathroom, but instead of heading to Julia, he went straight to the door. She thought about chasing after him, but she knew he would want to be left alone.

"He's going through a hard time," Julia explained in a whisper. "I think it's all getting on top of him."

"I'm not surprised," Alfie replied, taking the seat across from Julia. "His heart must be shattered."

"You know about that?"

Alfie assessed Julia with suspicion, his eyes creasing at the side. He sipped his pint before leaning back in his chair, an unsure smile on his lips.

"Do you?" he asked.

"He just told me everything," Julia explained. "It's so sad. He thought he'd found true love."

"I'm surprised he was that open with you," Alfie confessed, leaning in. "What did you put in the wine? I couldn't believe it when I found out."

"I didn't realise you were that close."

"We're not," Alfie said with a shrug. "Not really. I worked on a job for Mikey a couple of years back the last time I was in the country. He's a good guy. I like him."

Julia was glad that Mikey had at least one compassionate person in his life, and she was pleased it was Alfie. Even if they had never met before, she enjoyed being in his company, and she found she wanted to listen to him talk all afternoon. She thought about pressing him for stories of his travels, but she stopped herself, thinking it might be too forward.

"Your friends will probably be wondering where you are," Julia said, looking around the pub for the builders. "Oh, they've gone."

"They're not my friends," Alfie said without a hint of sadness. "They're probably outside smoking and cat-calling every poor woman who walks past.

It's not my scene."

"What is your '*scene*'?"

"Conversation," Alfie said as though it should have been obvious. "With a real human being about real things."

At that moment, Alfie's eyes danced down to Julia's chest. She realised that the bust-line of her dress had slipped down to reveal the top of her bra, so she quickly pulled it up. Her comfort in Alfie's presence switched to something entirely different, causing her cheeks to burn brightly. She looked up at him, embarrassed, but he looked as horrified as she did.

"I wasn't looking at -"

"I'm engaged," Julia said quickly, holding up the ring. "I'm flattered, but -"

"Honestly, I wasn't looking at that," Alfie said, his eyes darting down there again as he leaned in. "Your locket. What does the engraving say? I thought I -"

Julia looked down at Jessie's locket, and then up at Alfie. It sounded like the oldest trick in the book to get away with glancing at a woman's chest, but the sincere look on Alfie's face made her believe him. She rested her hand on the locket, the silver cool to the touch.

"It's from my foster daughter," Julia explained. "She gave it to me to mark our one-year anniversary of being together."

"The engraving," he repeated. "What does it say? What names are engraved on the front? I thought I saw something."

"My name," Julia said, looking down at the locket. "And my foster daughter's name. Jessie. Well, her full name is Jessika, but we all call her Jessie."

Alfie stared blankly at the locket for the longest time, beads of sweat gathering on his brow. When his eyes flicked up to hers, she saw something harrowing behind the glassy surface.

"Jessika spelt with a '*K*'?" he asked. "That's so - unusual."

"She's an unusual girl," Julia said, as she clipped the locket open to show him the pictures. "She's seventeen, but I'm telling you she's more mature than me when she wants to be. Other times, she's as immature as my nieces, but isn't that what being seventeen is all about?"

"Was she born in the year 2000?" Alfie asked, his eyes staring at the picture of Jessie. "May 25th, 2000?"

"How did you know?" Julia asked, snapping the locket shut, the feeling of familiarity being replaced by suspicion. "Why do you know that?"

Alfie reached into his pocket, his hands shaking more than Mikey's hand holding the glass of wine. He pulled out a tattered leather wallet before flipping it open and pulling out a white square. He looked down at it, his eyes full of the same confusion Julia felt. He passed it to her, revealing it to be a dog-eared Polaroid. The picture showed a newly born baby with a head of dark hair, the caption '*Baby Jessika*' scribbled in faded black pen underneath. Julia turned the picture over in her hands, the date of Jessie's birth scrawled on the back in the same handwriting.

"I had a sister called Jessika," Alfie said, his voice sounding strangely unlike his own. "Jessika with a '*K*'. I haven't seen her since our parents died seventeen years ago."

Julia stared down at the picture, her heart writhing in her chest. She looked up at Alfie, and then at the baby; she saw Jessie in both.

The walls began to close in around her, and her throat sealed at the top. She tried to speak, to scream, to make any noise, but nothing came forward. Her phone vibrated and rang loudly in her handbag, making her jump and drop the picture onto the table. Instead of pressing Alfie, she scrambled for her phone. When she saw Jessie's name and picture on the display, she suddenly found her words.

"*Hello*?" Julia called into the phone, her voice shaky.

"Where are you?" Jessie cried. "I thought you were taking me on a driving lesson at twelve? It's twenty past. I'm bored."

Julia stared at Alfie, who was staring at the phone; he knew who she was talking to.

"I'm on my way home," Julia said quickly before hanging up and throwing her phone back into her bag. "I need to go."

"Was that her?" Alfie cried, suddenly standing up. "Was that Jessie? I've seen her all over the village, and I knew - I *knew* who she was, but it felt too far-fetched to be true."

Julia stood up and slung her bag over her shoulder. She stared at Alfie as he looked at her, expectant and full of questions.

"I need to go," she repeated.

Before Alfie could say another word, Julia ran to her car, not daring to breathe until she was speeding towards her cottage.

CHAPTER 10

E arly the next morning, Julia found herself shivering outside a motorway service station before the sun had even risen. Cupping her hands to her face to warm them with her breath, she watched every car pass by, her anxiety growing with each passing vehicle.

When Kim Drinkwater's bright yellow Fiat Cinquecento careened into the car park, almost hitting four cars in the process, Julia did not know if she was happy or not to see Jessie's social worker.

After parking wonkily in the middle of two empty spaces, Kim tumbled out of her car, dropping a thick file of paperwork in the process. She gathered it up and stuffed it into an orange knitted bag, which matched her bright orange maxi dress and similarly-hued frosted eyeshadow.

Despite the nature of their meeting, Kim approached Julia with a beaming grin as her orange Crocs slapped against the damp tarmac.

"Can't say I've been awake this early in a while," Kim announced jovially as she looped through Julia's arm and pulled her into the service station. "Let's get warmed up. This cold weather gives me the willies."

The service station was filled with long-distance lorry drivers who looked like they had been driving for most of the night. Heads turned as Kim flounced towards the coffee shop, her rubber shoes slapping the tiles with each clumsy step.

"I'm dying for some caffeine," Kim proclaimed when they reached the counter of the small coffee shop. "And something sweet. *Muffins*! What flavour do I get?"

Julia could not bring herself to create small talk. She had one thing on her mind, and one thing only:

Alfie. She had spent the previous night unable to look Jessie in the eye, the possibilities and scenarios burning around in her mind. Even though she had retired to bed early, she had stayed up most of the night staring at the ceiling trying to piece together the truth. One of her final thoughts before she finally drifted off was that Alfie could be a stalker who had found out all of this information and concocted the whole story to get money from Julia.

As she watched Kim pluck each of the flavoured muffins from the display to sniff them, Julia peered down into Jessie's thick file, knowing the answers she craved were held between those pages.

After Kim ordered a large Frappuccino with two extra shots of coffee, three extra pumps of syrup, and artificial sweetener, they took the table on the edge of the coffee shop, which opened up into the food court-style dining of the service station.

"I always loved these places as a little girl," Kim said as she ripped the heads off four packets of sugar. "*Shhh*! Don't tell the slimming club. I put on weight again last week, but what they don't know won't hurt them."

Julia looked at the three muffins Kim had chosen, her stomach turning. Not because she was thinking about her weight, but because she was too nervous to even think about eating. She looked once again at the file, one simple answer able to turn her entire life upside down in a matter of moments.

"You know why I asked to meet you," Julia whispered, looking around the service station, even though she had purposefully picked the location for its distance from the village. "Do you remember what I asked you over the phone?"

"Ah, yes," Kim said, uninterested in what Julia had to say and more interested in unpeeling the first of her three muffins. "The man claiming to be Jessika's brother."

Kim bit into the muffin, her eyelids fluttering as though it was the first bite of something sweet she had taken in years. She chewed the mouthful before plucking the large, tattered file from her bag. Julia had seen it before, but she had never looked inside, even though Kim had told her on numerous occasions that she had permission to do so if she wanted. She had preferred Jessie's past to come from her lips and not the perspective of social workers, but now that something so big was up in the air, she needed to see the facts in writing.

"Is it true?" Julia pushed. "Does Jessie have a brother?"

Kim dropped the heavy file onto the table.

Before opening it, she took another bite of the muffin. Smearing chocolate on the front page, she opened it up and stamped her finger down on the top page.

"I'm afraid it's not as simple as that," Kim said with a sigh, one eye still on the muffin. "As you can see, Jessie's file started a little after her first birthday in 2001. I'd never noticed until you called me yesterday. I've been her social worker since she was six, but I never went that far back."

"Where's the rest?" Julia urged.

"Destroyed," Kim said with another sigh. "I asked some of the girls at work, and Pauline remembered a fire destroying a good chunk of our records just after the millennium. Jessie's files must have been in there, and this is when they were restarted."

"Didn't you have copies?" Julia asked. "Computer back-ups?"

"We'd only just come out of the nineties," Kim chuckled through a mouthful. "We barely had working pens, never mind a central computer database."

"And there's nothing about a brother in there?" Julia asked, wanting to rip the file from Kim to comb over every page. "No mention of an '*Alfie*'?"

"Not that I've found," Kim said with a shrug. "Although I only skimmed. My dad made a lovely curry last night, and I couldn't resist. I'm back living with him since I broke up with my last man. How's your Barker doing?"

"He's good," Julia snapped. "Is there any way of finding out if this is true?"

"There was Janie," Kim said, tapping her finger against her chin, which was now covered in gooey gloss thanks to her muffin. "She was Jessika's social worker before me. She'd probably know."

"Are you still in contact?" Julia urged, edging forward in her plastic chair. "Where is she?"

"Dead," Kim replied flatly. "Terrible incident with a curling iron and a bathtub, but the less said about that, the better. She was Jessika's social worker from birth, and then I took over."

"And there's no one else who you work with who remembers?" Julia asked, almost begging. "No one at all?"

"I did put the word around, but most people only know Jessika for her troubled ways," Kim explained as she flicked through the file. "Jumping from foster home to foster home, never settling for more than a couple of weeks. Setting fires, stealing things, fighting with the other children. She could never behave."

Julia's mind blurred. She had come here expecting to find out the definitive truth either way, but with Kim not having an answer, she could not focus her thoughts.

"Please tell me this," Julia said, trying to steady her voice as she stared into Kim's eyes. "Is it possible this man, Alfie, could really be Jessie's brother?"

Kim bit into her muffin once again as she pondered the question. After swallowing, she went to take another bite, but Julia rested her hand on Kim's arm to stop her.

"It's possible," Kim said finally. "Jessika's parents died in a terrible car accident from what I know. When babies go into care, their names are usually changed, but because she hadn't been taken away from her parents, they probably didn't see the point. If she'd had a brother, they would have been separated. You said this man was in his late twenties? All the more reason to split him up from a baby. Nobody ever wants to take siblings as a duo, especially when there's such an age gap. I did a search for an '*Alfie Rice*' in the database, but he could have changed his name along the way. Does he look like Jessika?"

"I'm sorry?"

"Does the man look like her?" Kim repeated as she reached out for her second muffin. "I usually find that's a good way to tell."

"He does," Julia replied bluntly. "A lot. I'm going to go."

"You won't mind if I stay here, will you?" Kim asked, her eyes firmly on her sweet treats. "I've only just got warm, and these are too good to pass up."

Julia did not bother to reply. She hurried towards her car and jumped inside. After turning on the engine, she switched on the heaters and waited with her fingers clenched tightly around the cold steering wheel.

As she stared at the sun struggling to break through the murky sky, she thought about how a part of her did not want to return to Peridale. A large van passed by inches from her car. When she spotted a newspaper logo on the side, an idea sprung to mind. It was so obvious, and yet she could not believe she had not thought of it before.

She scrambled in her bag, pulled out her phone, and opened up the web browser. After almost a minute of loading, the search engine appeared on the screen. After a deep breath, she typed '*Jessika Rice Car Accident*'. Thousands of results instantly sprung up, but the first one, a link to a newspaper article from the year 2000, caught her attention. The link took her to the *Blackpool Gazette* website. The headline made her stomach turn:

'TRAGIC MOTORWAY SMASH LEAVES CHILDREN ORPHANED.'

Julia closed her eyes before she continued reading. She felt as though she was reading something she should not have been. If Jessie did not know about having other siblings, she had not read the article either. If she had not needed to see the truth, she would have clicked right off the report, but for Jessie's sake, she needed the answers, so she continued reading:

'On Sunday, August 18th, a tragic car accident on the M55 resulted in the deaths of six people, one of those being Patrick Kennedy, who the police believe to have caused the fatal pile-up. Kennedy, a forty-six-year-old long-distance lorry driver and a resident of Dublin, Ireland, crashed his lorry through the central barrier and straight into oncoming traffic. Eyewitnesses claim to have seen Kennedy asleep at the wheel moments before the crash.

Among the victims were parents Olivia and Brett Rice, both thirty years old and residents of Blackpool who were travelling back from Skegness after a family holiday. Their two children, Alfred and Jessika, aged

*ten-years-old and three-months respectively,
were both in the back seats, but they
luckily survived the impact.'*

Julia stopped reading when the article diverted into the other victims of the accident. She locked her phone, unable to look at her screen anymore. Alfie was telling the truth, and that was all that mattered.

Against all the odds, he had turned up in Peridale for a building job and unknowingly found a sister he had been separated from for seventeen years. The thought of such a reunion made Julia want to jump for joy and sing from the rooftops, but a selfish voice in the back of her mind wanted to keep Jessie for herself, to preserve what they had in amber forever.

"Stop it, Julia," she whispered to herself as she pushed down the handbrake. "This isn't about you."

JULIA DROVE SLOWLY BACK TO PERIDALE, her hands and feet working on autopilot while the details of the article raced through her mind. Jessie had never shared anything about her parents because she claimed not to know anything other than how they died, but now that Julia knew their names, her history suddenly felt a lot more real.

Somehow along the way, she came up with a

plan: first, she would find Alfie to question him further about what he knew, and then she would find Jessie to tell her the truth. She had no idea how either situation would unfold but keeping the information to herself was only going to complicate things further.

The sun had risen, and the day had begun by the time Julia arrived in Peridale. A quick glance at her watch let her know she had just enough time to sneak back home, bake something to sell at the café, and open up for the day. When she spotted the police cars and crime scene tape strung across the opening of Mulberry Lane, Julia knew it would not be that simple. When she spotted Barker talking to DS Christie on the other side of the tape, her heart sank.

After parking wonkily on the kerb, Julia jumped out of her car and ran towards the tape. Ignoring the uniformed officers' protests, Julia ducked underneath and ran to Barker.

"What's happened?" she cried, looking around the street as police combed the area.

"I wondered how long it would be until *you* turned up," DS Christie replied with a roll of his eyes. "Who let her through? This is a *crime scene*, people. Authorised personnel *only*."

Before Julia could ask more questions, she noticed that the window in the door of Pretty Petals had been smashed. As the pieces slotted together, she realised the police activity concentrated around the flower shop.

"Suspected burglary gone wrong," DS Christie explained when he noticed Julia's eyes homing in on the shop. "Did you know her?"

Julia looked up at Barker, and then at the shop again. Two men carried out a stretcher with a red blanket covering a body.

"Harriet?" The name escaped Julia's lips before she had a second to think. "Harriet Barnes is *dead*?"

"Stabbed in the neck with her own gardening scissors," DS Christie announced coldly as he hooked his thumbs through the belt-straps of his trousers. "Poor thing must have been working late last night when someone smashed the window to rob the place. I bet they didn't even know she was there, so they panicked and stabbed her."

The two men carried Harriet into the back of an ambulance before slamming the doors shut.

"She has a cat," Julia found herself saying. "At her cottage. It'll need taking care of."

DS Christie scribbled down the detail on his notepad before turning to the shop.

"The flowers, Barker," Julia whispered, nudging him in the side when DS Christie walked towards the shop as he snapped on latex gloves. "This is connected. You know it."

"I tried telling him," Barker whispered back. "But he won't listen. What did she say to you when you talked to her?"

Julia cast her mind back to their conversation. Julia had always liked Harriet, so she felt guilty that their last exchange had been a frosty one.

"She didn't know who'd bought those specific flowers that were left at the scene," Julia said, almost to herself. "But if she's been murdered, she must have figured it out and confronted the person who bought them."

"We find the person who bought the flowers -"

"And we find the culprit," Julia jumped in, her mind suddenly switching to her early morning meeting. "Barker, there's something important I need to tell you. Are you needed here, or can we go home to talk?"

"I only came because Christie called me," Barker said. "I'm here unofficially. We might be interrupting Jessie's reunion with her friend if we go back now. How about your café? I know it's early, but I'm sure you'll have customers lining up when word of this spreads."

"Reunion?" Julia asked, grabbing Barker's arm as the words caught in her throat. "What reunion?"

"One of the builders," Barker replied with a shrug. "He said he knew Jessie and wanted to say hello."

"What did he look like?"

Barker thought for a moment as he stared curiously at Julia. She nodded to rush him, her mind racing once again.

"Has something happened?" Barker asked, his hands landing on Julia's shoulders. "You've gone pale."

"What did the builder look like, Barker?"

"I don't know," Barker said with a shake of his head. "He was about my height. Dark hair and eyes. He had some tattoos, and -"

Not needing to hear another word, Julia grabbed Barker's hand and dragged him towards the blue and white tape. They ducked underneath just as the forensic van pulled up.

"Are you going to tell me what's going on?" Barker cried as they sped up the winding lane towards their cottage, passing the building site at lightning speed. "Who is he, Julia?"

Julia tried to explain everything to Barker, but

the words would not form into sentences in her brain. She screeched to a halt in front of her cottage right behind Alfie's motorbike.

Without even taking the keys out of the ignition, Julia cranked up her handbrake, burst out of her car and down the garden path. She flung open her cottage door, stopping in her tracks when she saw Jessie and Alfie standing together in the hallway. Jessie was holding the Polaroid picture in her hands, her dark brows tensed firmly over her eyes.

"Jessie?" Julia called out, her voice shaking. "Let me explain -"

But Jessie was not interested in hearing anything Julia had to say. She looked down at the picture, and then up at Alfie. The picture fell out of her hands, and she barged past Julia and out of the cottage, almost knocking her to the ground in the process.

"It's her," Alfie mumbled. "It's really *her*."

Unable to be the one to comfort him, Julia spun on her heels, almost banging into Barker as he made his way up the garden path. She ran into the road and stood between the motorbike and her still-running car. She looked up and down the winding lane, but Jessie was nowhere to be seen.

"Is someone going to explain to me what's going on?" Barker cried.

CHAPTER 11

J ulia did not see Jessie in the days following her discovery of Alfie. She did not know if it was because she was angry at Julia for not telling her, or scared of the truth, but Jessie had been hiding at Billy's and refused to see or speak to Julia. Even though she had taken her some clean clothes, Jessie had declined to come to the door to show Julia that she was even still alive.

Julia had also not seen or heard from Alfie. She

had searched for the builder, but he had checked out of the B&B and had not been seen around the village. She knew Jessie running away and hiding must have felt like a rejection, but because he was no longer around, Julia could not explain to him that it was Jessie's way of dealing with things.

Harriet's murder had been just enough to keep Julia distracted from the drama happening in her family. It was all people had talked about in her café since the morning of the murder, but she had heard no one linking it to Shane's death. Aside from in the context of '*another death so soon after that builder*', no other residents aside from Julia suspected a connection. The narrative of a '*burglary gone wrong*' had circulated the village at whirlwind speed, no doubt thanks to DS Christie. Despite having no evidence to prove it was such a thing, he seemed set on his theory, and nothing Julia could say would budge him.

Julia had tried her best to discover who had bought the flowers, or even where they had gone, but she had come up with nothing. Billy had asked the other builders if any of them had seen the flowers while they were laid at the site, but nobody had. If not for the vague photograph on her phone, Julia might have believed the flowers had been nothing more than a figment of her overactive imagination.

By Wednesday afternoon, Julia was leaning against the counter in her café, flicking through the bridal magazines but barely paying any attention. She smiled at the odd customers when they came in for their orders, but she felt as far from smiling as any woman could.

After the builders, minus Alfie and Billy, came into the café for their lunch, Julia was glad to be clearing up their mess to give her something to do. When Katie pushed open the door with the end of Vinnie's pram, Julia's first genuine smile of the day appeared.

"Go and see your big sister," Katie said, reaching into the pram to grab Vinnie. "He's looking more and more like your father as the days pass."

Julia held her brother, who was heavier than he looked. He frowned up at her, his hazel eyes taking in his older sister. His wispy brown hair had started to thicken, and despite being a baby, Katie was right about him looking like her father. As she stared at her brother, she realised this would have been the age Jessie was when her parents died. The thought unsettled her, so she passed Vinnie back, playing it off as needing to get back to sweeping up the crumbs under the tables.

"I've just come from the mother and baby group with Sue," Katie announced as she placed Vinnie back in his pram. "I didn't even know Peridale had one, but it turns out the village hall has all sorts for tots. We've signed up for a music class next week."

"With my sister?" Julia asked with an arched brow. "My sister Sue?"

"The very same," Katie replied with a shrill giggle. "Who knew we had so much in common? We've been spending so much time together since we chatted about Candy, although just between us, I'm sick and tired of having that diva at my house."

"Oh?" Julia said, resting on her broom as she stared at Katie. "Has something happened?"

"Not exactly," Katie said with a sigh as she planted herself in one of the seats. "But she's taken over the place! Your father can't go into his study, she's taken the biggest guest room, which is where I liked watching my shows when your father was watching his sports. And the *arguments*! Oh, the *constant* arguing! It's not healthy for Vinnie hearing all of that. Your father and I never argue, and now it's constant. I'm leaving the house every chance I get because seeing her face is making me want to tell her to leave. I can't do that though, can I? We're old friends."

Julia thought back to the comment Candy had made about them being '*acquaintances*' rather than '*friends*', but she decided not to mention anything. If Katie found out Candy was using her for free accommodation, it would likely start a war, the likes of which Peridale had never seen.

"Candy and Harold argue a lot?" Julia asked casually as she carried on sweeping. "I wouldn't have thought Harold was the type."

"He's not," Katie said with a sigh. "But *she* is. She's always been like that. She could start an argument with a brick wall if she thought it was looking at her funny. She once started a screaming match with me at a photo shoot because she said I'd stolen her hair extensions. They had to shut the whole thing down because she was hysterical and out of control. I *had* stolen her hair extensions, but that's not the point. I'd forgotten mine, so I needed something. They were cheap ratty things anyway, so I ended up pulling them right out of my head and throwing them at her. You should have seen her face! That was the last time I saw her. We were friends before that, so when she called me to ask if I was still living in Peridale, I decided to let it slide. Be the bigger person, ya know? Now that I'm a mother, I didn't want to hold onto those old childish arguments. We were both different people back then, but I don't think she's grown out of it."

"Sounds like she has an anger problem," Julia suggested as she gathered up the empty plates, the image of Candy holding a bloodied brick after whacking Shane not difficult to conjure up. "What do they argue about?"

"Anything and everything," Katie said with a roll of her eyes as she pushed her blonde hair away from her face. "It was a pair of shoes last night. She thought he'd moved them. Turns out Hilary had moved them because she'd just kicked them off at the front door. We have a place for everything at the manor, especially now that Hilary is walking with that crutch. It's not safe to leave things on the floor. I have to be so careful with Vinnie's toys, but Candy didn't care. When she was finished unloading her anger on poor Harold, she turned on Hilary, but you know what Hilary is like. I thought she was going to hit Candy with her stick. I think she might have done it if she didn't need it to stand upright. Part of me wished she had. I feel so awful saying all of this. We go so far back, but I don't have the energy for all of that anymore."

"And Harold never bites back?"

"*Never!*" Katie exclaimed, her voice squeaking. "Not until this morning, anyway. Oh, you should have been there. The house shook when Candy slammed the front door. I couldn't believe what I overheard."

Julia stopped gathering the plates and turned to Katie, eager to know what she had overheard. Katie looked around her as though expecting Candy to be standing behind her, but when she saw that the coast was clear, she leaned in with a concealed grin.

"Candy started on one of her rants as usual," Katie whispered. "I wasn't listening because you learn to tune it out, but Harold bit back. When I heard his voice raise, my ears pricked up. They have the bedroom next to mine, so I put my ear up against the wall. Your father thought I was over the top, but I wanted to hear what he had to say. Poor man barely speaks. He said he knew what she'd done with - well, I didn't hear what he said properly. Vinnie sneezed. It sounded like he said '*shade*', but I don't know what that means."

"Shane?" Julia jumped in.

"It might have been!" Katie cried, clicking her fingers together. "He said *I know what you did with Shane, and I'm not going to put up with it this time. I'm tired'*. And then he slapped her. Sounded really hard. It was so loud it made me hold my breath. Then, I heard Candy scream and storm out. The door slammed, and she drove off. I haven't seen her since. Part of me hopes she doesn't come back."

Julia sat down across from Katie, her mind racing once again. She had needed confirmation of Harold knowing about Candy's affair to think of him as a suspect, and now that she had it, she was unsure of what to think.

"If I told you I saw Candy kissing a man in an alley that wasn't her husband, what would you say?" Julia asked carefully.

"I'd say that sounds like Candy," Katie said with a chuckle. "She'll never change. Even back then, she was married to Harold and messing around with the male models behind his back. I never said anything because I'm a good friend, but we all knew what she was up to. She never even tried to hide it. We all thought he knew too and he ignored it because she was a model and so beautiful."

"I saw her kissing Shane in an alley," Julia whispered, her voice shaking. "It was the day before Shane died."

"You mean the builder?" Katie gasped. "The bald man who died? He doesn't seem like her type from what I've heard. Are you sure?"

"Positive," Julia confirmed. "I saw them with my own two eyes hours before Shane was murdered. If Harold knew, it means -"

"Either of them could have killed him!" Katie exclaimed, her hand planting down on the table. "Candy could have killed him to keep the affair a secret, and Harold could have killed him to teach them both a lesson!"

Julia was impressed. Katie gave off the impression she was a bimbo, but Julia had always suspected that she had brains underneath it all if she applied herself.

"*Valentine's Day!*" Katie exclaimed. "The day after Candy and Harold arrived at the manor! That was their biggest row before this one today. She vanished and was gone all day. Your father put on the most romantic meal for us in the dining room, but Harold spent the night alone in his room. She crawled back in the early hours of the morning, and he asked where she'd been, but she wouldn't tell him. She stormed out again. We heard him crying. I wanted to talk to him, but your father told me to leave him. Poor guy was probably embarrassed that she'd stood him up."

"Did she have any roses with her?" Julia asked. "A dozen red roses?"

Katie thought about it for a moment, but she shrugged, apparently unable to remember. Julia was about to delve deeper, but she stopped herself when she noticed Billy hurrying across the village green with a plastic bag in his hand.

"Watch the café," Julia said, already springing up. "I'll be back in two seconds."

Katie's protests followed her through the door, but Julia was too focussed. She called and waved to Billy who did not look like he was going to stop at first. When he finally did, she sensed his reluctance to talk.

"I've just bought Jessie her favourite wrap from the chicken shop," Billy said, holding up the bag. "It was a long walk, so I can't talk too long. It'll go cold."

"I won't keep you," Julia said. "I just wanted to know how she's doing. She won't answer my calls."

Billy looked down at his feet and huffed out his chest.

"She won't talk to me, Miss S," Billy whispered, looking from side to side. "Hasn't said a word since she came to mine. Won't even tell me what's happened. I only know about Alfie because you told me. I keep trying, but it's like she's in a coma."

"It's probably the shock," Julia said, her worst

fears realised. "Is she eating?"

"Little bits," Billy said, looking down at the bag. "I thought her favourite chicken wrap with extra mayo would be too good to resist."

"You're a good kid, Billy," Julia said, patting him on the shoulder. "Tell her to call me, okay? I miss her."

"I'll try, Miss S," Billy said with a shrug as he backed away. "I can't promise anything."

"I know," she said with a smile. "Just try."

Julia turned to head back to her cottage, but a familiar motorbike parked outside the B&B caught her attention; a plan instantly formed in her mind.

"Billy?" Julia called after him before he vanished down a side street. "Get Jessie to my cottage tonight around eight."

"But, Miss S, she won't -"

"Please," Julia cut in, her eyes begging him. "Please. I need to fix this."

Billy sighed and nodded before slipping out of view. Julia glanced back to the café, her heart fluttering when she saw that Katie was behind the counter attempting to serve someone. Julia knew she should run back to save her, but this was more important than her business. Not wanting to waste a single second, Julia sprinted up to the B&B. She was relieved when she saw that the motorbike was the same one that had pulled up outside her café on the day Alfie had come to Peridale.

Instead of ringing the doorbell to the B&B, Julia let herself in. The chimes above the door announced her entrance, but nobody ran into the hallway to stop her. The strong smell of incense floated in from the sitting room, leading Julia inside.

She was surprised to see Alfie lying on the couch with Evelyn hovering over him, her eyes clenched as her hands vibrated over his chest. The curtains were closed, the only light coming from the candles dotted around the room. Julia watched Evelyn hover up and down his body for a moment before clearing her throat to broadcast her presence.

"Hello, Julia," Evelyn said without opening her eyes or looking in her direction. "I won't be a second. I'm just cleansing Alfie here. He's got a lot of built up stress, and I can't have that in my home."

Alfie opened his eyes and attempted to sit up, but Evelyn's palm reached out and pushed his face back into the couch. She continued to hover her hands over his body until she appeared satisfied. When she was done, she opened her eyes and blinked into the dark with a content smile.

"Done," Evelyn said with a firm nod. "Stay out

of direct sunlight for the next hour, and wear this."

Evelyn pulled a crystal pendant from within her kaftan and draped it around Alfie's neck as he sat upright. As though sensing that they needed to talk, Evelyn slipped out of the room, leaving them alone.

"Where have you been?" Julia asked, unsure of where to start. "I've been looking for you."

"I needed a couple of days away from here," Alfie explained as he leaned on his knees. "I wasn't sure I was going to come back, but I couldn't not try."

Julia appreciated Alfie returning. She could not understand half of what he was going through, but she did know that she could try to be a bridge between the past and the present.

"I'm sorry," Julia said firmly. "I should have been better. I was thinking only of myself and Jessie. I didn't take your feelings into consideration, and that was selfish."

"She's your kid," Alfie said with a smile as he stood up and stretched out. "You clearly love her a lot. I would have done the same."

Alfie gave her a look that let her know she did not need to apologise again. It only made her feel worse for suspecting him as a liar in the first place.

"I'm scared, Julia," Alfie whispered, taking a step

towards her in the dark, the flickering candles warming his face. "I'd given up hope. What do I do?"

"Come to dinner at my cottage," Julia said. "At eight. Jessie will be there. All you can do is try. You've had seventeen years to miss her, but she's only known of your existence for two days. It will take time."

Alfie nodded as he looked down at the floor. Julia could tell he had a thousand questions about his sister.

"What's she like?" he asked.

"You'll find out," Julia said as she took a step back towards the door. "Tonight, at eight. You'll see how special she is."

Leaving Alfie in the dark, Julia walked out of the B&B and headed back to the café. She knew it was a risk expecting Jessie to turn up, and even though she was unpredictable, Julia knew her as well as any person could. All Jessie had ever wanted was a family; she was not going to reject her only living flesh and blood.

"*Julia*!" Katie shrieked when she returned to the café, feeling more optimistic than when she'd left it. "The coffee machine has gone crazy! *Help*!"

CHAPTER 12

J ulia had been pacing her kitchen for the past twenty minutes, but she could not seem to stand still. She stopped to check on the chicken roasting in the oven, the heat hitting her in the face. When she saw that it was nearly finished, she resumed her pacing, her eyes on the cat clock above the fridge.

"What if she doesn't come?" Julia asked Barker, who had been sitting at the counter with his typewriter watching her since she had started pacing. "What if this is it? She's never going to be the same again."

"This is a good thing for her," Barker said, his fingers lazily hitting the keys, his attention divided as he worked on the first chapter of his next book. "But you're right, things will probably never be the same again."

"What if she hates me?"

"Why would she hate you?" Barker cried. "You've done more for her than anyone else. Look at that locket she gave you to show you how much she loves you."

Julia's hand rested on the locket, but she could not bring herself to look down at it. She stopped to ignite the gas rings under the pans of vegetables waiting to be boiled before continuing with her pacing.

"I feel so sick," Julia whined. "Why does nothing ever go smoothly?"

"Because that's life," Barker exclaimed as he pulled the paper from the typewriter. "And this is rubbish."

He screwed up the paper and tossed it onto the pile of similarly screwed-up paper on the floor next to him. Mowgli walked past and batted it with his paw, but even he could not muster the energy to be excited by the writing.

"I'm sorry," Julia said, resting a hand on her forehead. "I shouldn't be putting this on you."

"You should," Barker said as he fed another fresh sheet of paper into the typewriter. "This is what being in a relationship is all about. You talk, I listen, and I try to help. I might not be very good at it, like I'm not very good at writing right now, but I'll always do what I can. I'm nervous too, but I'm trying not to let it get on top of me. It's a lot to take in at once."

The oven beeped, making Julia jump. She checked the chicken once more before turning the heat right down to keep it warm. The clock ticked past five minutes to eight, making her nerves bubble up again.

"She's not coming," Julia moaned. "Oh, Barker. What do I do?"

Barker slid off his stool and pulled her into his chest. He stroked the back of her hair, the only noise coming from the water in the pans as they began to boil.

"Calm down," he whispered soothingly. "Give her a chance. You know what she's like. She's late for everything."

Julia nodded, wanting to believe Barker. She imagined Jessie sitting in Billy's room, silent and staring at the wall as he tried to force her to get up. Was Alfie at the B&B doing something similar? Barker pulled away from the hug and turned to grab a piece of paper from his open briefcase on the counter. He looked down at it, his teeth biting into the corner of his bottom lip.

"There's something I need to tell you," Barker said. "I was going to wait until afterwards, but I think it's best we go into this knowing everything there is to -"

A knock at the front door stopped Barker mid-sentence. They both jumped, their eyes darting to the hallway. He looked down at the paper again before shoving it back into his briefcase. Instead of leaving it open, he snapped it shut and scrambled the lock.

"What was it?" Julia asked, her eyes still on the hallway. "What should I know?"

"It can wait," he assured her with an encouraging smile. "Maybe you should see who's at the door?"

Julia stared at him blankly for a moment, almost forgetting what was going on. When the aroma of roast chicken tickled her nostrils, she sprang into life and pulled her apron over her head. She smoothed out the creases in her simple knitted jumper before hurrying for the door.

She checked her reflection in the mirror on the way to the door, her curly hair pulled off her face into a loose ponytail. She wondered if she should have put more effort in, not that she thought it would make a difference to how things were going to go. After taking a deep breath, Julia pulled open the door, a smile plastered across her face. The smile faltered when she saw that it was Jessie and Billy, and not Alfie who had been knocking.

"*Jessie*!" Julia exclaimed, throwing back the door. "Why did you knock? This is your home."

Jessie tucked her damp hair behind her ears and shrugged. She looked as though she had just showered, and she was wearing the fresh clothes Julia had bagged up and dropped off at Billy's house.

"Come in," Julia said when she realised that Jessie was waiting to be invited inside. "Dinner is nearly ready."

Jessie plodded into the hallway, her eyes firmly on the ground. Billy offered an apologetic smile as he followed her in. He had convinced her to come, and that was all she had asked of him. One piece of the jigsaw was in place, Julia only hoped the second piece would turn up soon.

After kicking off her shoes, Jessie walked into the sitting room where a fire was waiting for her. She sat in her usual spot next to the fireplace and pulled her legs up against her chest. Resting her head against the armrest, she stared blankly into the dancing flames, her gaze that of a broken girl.

"This is what she's been like," Billy whispered as he pulled off his coat. "I don't know what to do. I practically had to drag her here."

Barker appeared with a bottle of beer for Billy, and the two retreated into the kitchen. Julia watched Jessie, wishing she knew what to do or say to make everything better again. Knowing she had to try something, Julia crept into the sitting room and perched on the edge of the coffee table. She reached out and rested a hand on Jessie's leg, causing her to flinch. Julia immediately pulled it away, her heart hurting.

"Thanks for coming," Julia said softly. "Mowgli has missed you."

As though he heard his name, Mowgli trotted into the room. He jumped up onto the arm of the chair and stared at Jessie. When she did not look back, he patted her cautiously with his paw and meowed. To Julia's relief, she looked away from the fire and stroked Mowgli's head, the corners of her lips pricking up.

"I'm sorry," Julia said, the words tumbling out of her mouth. "I'm sorry about all of this."

"Why are you sorry?" Jessie replied, her brows tensing over her eyes as she tickled Mowgli's scalp. "What did you do?"

Julia was so glad to hear Jessie talk, a smile spread from ear to ear. She edged forward, reaching out to rest her hand on Jessie's leg again. This time, she did not flinch, so Julia kept it there; she really wanted to pull Jessie into a tight hug, but she knew that might scare her away.

"I didn't want you to find out like that," Julia said. "When Alfie told me, I didn't know what to think. I didn't know if it was true, so I spoke to Kim. I was on my way back to tell you everything, but Alfie got here first."

"I'm used to you sneaking around," Jessie said flatly. "I found those condoms you gave Billy. He said you'd told him not to tell me, but I got it out of him."

"Oh, Jessie -"

"You care," Jessie jumped in, her blank eyes darting up to Julia for the first time. "You care more than anyone else ever has." Jessie paused to exhale.

"Why is this happening now when everything was going perfectly? Why didn't he turn up when I was crying myself to sleep in the children's homes, or when I was shivering on a street corner somewhere, a cup for change at my feet? I don't get it."

Julia did not have the answers to Jessie's questions. She tried to think of a way she could frame the situation into the positive one she knew it was deep down, but she knew where Jessie's feelings were coming from.

"When my mum died, I used to think the same thing," Julia said, her eyes drifting up to the framed picture of her on the mantelpiece. "I would think *'why isn't my mum here for me?'*. I would cry myself to sleep after the biggest moments in my life because she wasn't there to see it. Life is cruel, Jessie, but you know that. You've suffered more than most, but that's over now, and you don't have to cry yourself to sleep over this. You've just found out you have a brother, and he's alive, and he's here."

"What's he like?" Jessie asked, her question mirroring that of Alfie's in the B&B yesterday.

"He's nice," Julia replied quickly. "He's really sweet and thoughtful, just like his sister. I won't pretend to know everything about him, and I think it's best you find out from him. You need to remember he's feeling everything you're feeling right now. Look at this from his perspective. He had a baby sister who he was separated from when he was just ten-years-old. It's only by chance that you've ended up in the same place at the same time, so you need to take this chance. I'm not sure I believe in fate, but you gave me this locket, and that's what unravelled all of this. That sounds like fate to me."

Jessie smiled as Mowgli crawled carefully into her lap. Julia's nerves eased, but they spiked up seconds later when a second knock at the door shuddered through the cottage. Mowgli jumped up and flew into the hallway, running past Barker and Billy who had appeared in the doorway.

"Maybe we should go?" Barker said, planting a hand on Billy's shoulder. "Leave you to it."

"No!" Jessie cried, jumping up. "You're the three most important people in my life. I want - no - I *need* you here."

Jessie walked over to Billy, her hand wrapping tightly around his. Half hiding behind him, she trained her eyes on the door as though she could not bring herself to look away.

Pushing her own nerves to the side, Julia opened the door. Alfie was standing on the doorstep, a bunch of flowers in his hand, a frightened look on his face. He was wearing a black shirt under his beaten-up biker jacket. His dark hair was pushed back with some wax, but it still had the messy quality that Julia liked.

"Right on time," Julia announced brightly. "Please, come in."

Julia stepped aside, but Alfie did not immediately walk in. His eyes landed on Jessie, and he gulped as though he was trying to swallow a mouthful of glass. Julia cleared her throat, breaking him from his trance. He stepped into the cottage enough for Julia to close the door behind him. They were both here, but whatever was going to happen next was a mystery to her.

"These are for you," Alfie said, breaking the awkward silence as he offered the flowers to Julia. "I had to get them from the corner shop, but they're the nicest I could find."

"They're lovely," Julia said as she accepted the colourful bouquet. "Thank you."

"I didn't know if I should bring wine," Alfie said with a nervous laugh. "I've never done anything like this before."

"You're here," Julia said, patting him on the shoulder. "That's all that matters. Barker, why don't you show everyone through to the dining room while I get dinner ready? I hope you all like roast chicken."

Jessie dragged Billy into the dining room, her eyes firmly down. Alfie looked around the cottage, his awkwardness almost identical to Jessie's. He shrugged off his leather jacket and Julia hung it on the hat stand with the other coats.

"You like beer?" Barker asked after shaking Alfie's hand. "Go through, and I'll bring a bottle in."

Alfie walked over to the dining room door. He looked over his shoulder at Julia as though waiting for permission. She nodded with an encouraging smile, pushing him to venture inside.

Julia hurried into the kitchen and quickly put the flowers in a vase of water. The flowers were not a patch on Harriet's beautiful bouquets, but Julia appreciated the thought behind them. As she placed them on the corner of the counter, it suddenly hit her that no one in Peridale would experience Harriet's talents again. Knowing she could not let her mind dwell on such things tonight, she stuffed her hands into her oven mitts and pulled out the crispy roast chicken.

After quickly making gravy, Julia put five plates on the counter and plated up the vegetables. When she started to carve the succulent chicken, Jessie's laughter floated through from the dining room. Eager to know what she was missing out on, Julia rushed through the slices, almost tossing them onto the plates. With all five plates expertly balanced, she hurried into the dining room.

"And then when I got halfway up the side of the pyramid, the police helicopter started circling, and I was sure I was done for," Alfie said as he leaned into Jessie with his phone. "I'm banned from stepping foot in Egypt ever again, but I got some beautiful shots."

"You've been to so many places," Jessie said as she flicked through the pictures. "Where did you take this one?"

Julia placed the plates on the table, but Jessie and Alfie were so deep in their conversation, she might as well not have been there. Billy and Barker watched on silently as they sipped their beer, both of them looking as surprised as Julia felt. After hurrying back to fetch the gravy and cutlery, Julia took her place at the head of the table.

"I took that one just after I was let out of a Thai prison," Alfie said, his arm reaching around the back of Jessie's chair as he watched her flick through his pictures. "If you ever find yourself in Thailand, don't joke about the royal family in front of the police. My lawyer said I could have got fifteen years if they had been in a different mood. That was a wild week."

"Prison?" Julia called out as she carefully cut a piece of broccoli in half. "So, you've been arrested a lot?"

Jessie shot Julia a look that she knew meant '*why are you asking that?*' before looking back down at Alfie's phone, her dinner going unnoticed.

"You don't spend as many years travelling as I did and not get yourself in trouble along the way," Alfie said with a sheepish smile. "There are some crazy laws out there. I was arrested on a beach in Jamaica for wearing camouflage shorts. Who knew that was illegal there? I never really was a guidebook sort of guy."

"This is so cool," Jessie said, almost to herself as she flicked through the pictures. "You've been everywhere. I haven't even left the country."

"There's time for that," Alfie said as he took his phone back. "You're still young. You've got your entire life ahead of you. I didn't go on my first plane until I was eighteen when I was finally out of the system."

Alfie pulled his plate towards him before pouring gravy over his chicken. Jessie did the same, and Julia could tell that she was suddenly bursting with questions despite her earlier fear.

"You were in the system?" Jessie asked as Alfie passed the gravy to her. "For how long?"

"From the day they separated us," Alfie said, his fork pausing before it reached his mouth. "I still remember it like it was yesterday. They took us to an office in some council building, and they told that someone was going to foster you, but I was staying at the children's home. The other kids had told me that was going to happen, but I was adamant we were going to stay together. I wouldn't let go of you, so they had to pry you from my arms. I was only ten. They took you out of the room and promised that I would get to see you again, but I never did. I did try looking for you, Jessika."

"Everyone calls me Jessie," she jumped in. "Just Jessie."

"Jessie it is," he replied quickly. "That's what Dad used to call you."

Jessie's eyes darted down to her food. She moved her broccoli around on her plate, but she had yet to eat any of it. Julia glanced at Barker, who was watching her like a hawk as though he was going to swoop in and save her if he needed to.

"What were they like?" Jessie asked, her voice

barely above a whisper. "I don't know anything."

"They loved you," Alfie said quickly, his eyes darting down like Jessie's. "I know they tried so hard to have another baby. They wanted you so badly, and when you came along, you were perfect. They bought you the best of everything. Mum would push you around town all dressed up like you were a superstar. And Dad adored you. He called you his little princess. Princess Jessie. The day - the day *it* happened - we'd just been on holiday at the seaside. It was your first holiday. You loved the sand. I can still see your happy little face. Dad wanted to set off earlier to avoid the traffic, but Mum wanted to stay and soak up the last of the sun before it set. I used to think I should have known something bad was going to happen. I could have saved them if I'd told them to leave sooner. It was a miracle we came out alive. I had a broken ankle and arm, but your car seat saved you." Alfie paused and dropped his fork onto his plate before reaching out and grabbing Jessie's hand. "I promise I tried looking for you. They moved me to a half-way house when I was sixteen, and I spent months trying to track you down. I spoke to hundreds of people in the care system, and nobody could pin you down. We had no other family. Mum and Dad were only children, and their parents died when they were young too. I always wondered if that's why they were drawn to each other. When I was eighteen, I got out, and that's when I left the country. I had nothing and no one, so I just left. I always thought I'd bump into you in some market or museum. I never gave up hope that I'd see you again, I just never expected it to be here."

As Jessie stared down at Alfie's hand around hers, tears streamed silently down her face. Silence fell on the dining room, none of them eating. Julia wiped away her own tears as she resisted the urge to comfort Jessie.

"I always felt so alone," Jessie whispered. "I bounced from place to place, never settling in. I was always the odd one out. The freak with dead parents. I had no one, but I didn't even have hope that I would one day meet you because I didn't know you existed. I ran away from my last foster placement, and I slept rough for six months. It was the hardest time of my life, but then I found Julia. She doesn't believe in fate, but I think I do now. I found her, and she found me, and it's led me to finding you too. I don't know what it all means, but I'm happy. I'm scared, and I'm angry at the universe for putting me through everything to get here, but I'm happy."

Jessie pulled her hand away from Alfie's and

finally started eating her food. Alfie followed, but Julia, Barker, and Billy watched on in silence, none of them seeming to know how to act or what to say.

"What happens now?" Billy asked after the silence grew to an uncomfortable peak. "Are you staying in Peridale, or are you heading off after the build is finished? You told me you'd already booked your tickets to Mexico."

Alfie frowned at Billy as he chewed a mouthful of chicken. He washed it down with some beer before wiping his mouth with a napkin.

"That was before," Alfie said finally. "I don't know what's happening now. Jessika and - I mean - *Jessie* and I have a lot to talk about. There are seventeen years to catch up on."

"So, you *are* staying in Peridale then?" Billy pushed, his eyes narrowed suspiciously on Alfie. "It's a simple question, mate."

"It's hardly a simple situation," Alfie fired back, dropping his fork onto his plate. "What's with the questions? I thought we were friends."

"Like you said, things have changed," Billy said, his eyes narrowing further. "Jessie is my world. I don't want you upsetting her."

"Why would I upset her?" Alfie said with a stifled laugh. "She's my sister."

"Because you don't know her like I do," Billy shot back. "You don't know her like any of us do. None of us wants to see her go through any more crap."

"Billy -" Barker started.

"We don't *know* this guy!" Billy cried, his cheeks burning bright red. "He could be anyone under those tattoos."

"Shut up, Billy," Jessie muttered through gritted teeth. "Why are you doing this?"

"You were saying the same things earlier, babe!" Billy cried. "I'm only thinking of you. I just want to know what his intentions are. He can't have looked that hard to find you. It's not like you're not on social media now like the rest of us. I just want -"

"Get out," Jessie snarled. "Get out right now!"

"Babe -"

"*Go on!*" Jessie suddenly jumped up. "You're not thinking about me, you're thinking about yourself."

Billy opened and closed his mouth, but the protest did not come. He screwed up his napkin and tossed it on the table before matching Jessie in standing. He tried to meet her eyes, but she purposefully avoided looking at him.

"Fine," Billy said before sucking in air through his teeth. "If that's what you want, I'm gone."

After grabbing his beer bottle from the table, Billy slipped out of the dining room, the front door slamming loudly behind him. Jessie sat back down in her chair and resumed looking at her food. Julia and Barker exchanged a *'what was that about?'* glance, but Julia knew deep down. She had the same fears Billy had, but without the teenage hormones coursing through her body, she was able to keep them to herself for now.

"This is new to me too," Alfie said finally as he pushed his barely eaten food away from him. "It wasn't easy for me to come here. I've had seventeen years of wondering, and now this has landed on me. It's a lot to process."

"Just ignore him," Jessie mumbled as she resumed pushing her broccoli around. "He's such an idiot sometimes. I don't know why I bother with him."

The conversation soon turned back to stories of Alfie's travels, but Julia could not bring herself to stay fully engaged in listening. She had tuned into Billy's thoughts, and they were worrying her.

Candy's house would be finished in the coming months, and when it was, Alfie would be free to go where he wanted. With tickets booked to Mexico, he could jump on a plane and vanish from Jessie's life before he had even become a part of it. Julia searched the traveller's eyes as he told his stories, and she wondered if leaving that behind to build a relationship with his teenage sister was a realistic option for him. Peridale was not his home, and when his stay at the B&B was up, he would be homeless and jobless. If it came to that situation, Julia would offer him her couch in a heartbeat, but she knew for people like Alfie, he could quickly tire of that rooted life.

When the scraping of knives and forks ceased, Julia replaced their plates with hot apple pie and custard, which went down easier than her roast chicken and vegetables. When they were finished with dessert, they naturally drifted through to the hallway as the evening drew to a close.

"When will I see you again?" Jessie asked as they lingered by the door. "Tomorrow?"

"I can pick you up when I've finished at the building site?" Alfie offered as he reached for his leather jacket. "We'll go for a ride somewhere. Maybe go to the cinema or go for a meal. My treat. It will give us a chance to talk properly."

"Awesome," Jessie said, a grin from ear to ear. "I'll see you tomorrow, bro."

"You too, sis," Alfie said with a chuckle. "I don't

think I'll ever get used to saying that."

With that, Jessie retreated to her bedroom. Julia had no doubt she would immediately start texting Billy to ask him what his problem was; she just hoped she would go gently on him.

"I'll start washing up," Barker said, backing down the hallway as though he sensed that Julia wanted to talk to Alfie alone. "Call me if you need me."

When they were alone, they lingered silently by the door, neither of them seeming to know what to say. Julia had a thousand questions, but the last thing she wanted to do was scare Alfie off.

"Thanks for inviting me," Alfie said. "You were right about her being special. She's a great kid. She reminds me of me at that age."

"It's a difficult time for her," Julia said. "You know what it's like being a teenager."

"I do," Alfie agreed. "I'm not going to hurt her, Julia. I've dreamed of this moment for years. No matter what Billy thinks, I'm not just going to run away from this."

Julia believed that Alfie believed his words, but it was not enough for her. He had already disappeared once, even if he had returned. She thought about everything she knew of Alfie so far, and she did like the man, but there were a lot of unanswered questions, the biggest of them all relating to Shane's murder.

"Can I ask you something?" Julia whispered, taking a step closer to him. "Something I have been wondering about for a while?"

"Sure."

"Why was Shane strangling you at the B&B?" Julia asked. "What did you do that made him so angry?"

"Shane was a hot head," Alfie said. "But he wasn't all he seemed. It wasn't what I did, it was what I saw."

"And what did you see?"

Alfie assessed Julia with a peculiar smile; it made her feel like he thought she already knew.

"Let's just say Shane was in bed with someone he shouldn't have been," Alfie said as he zipped up his leather jacket. "But it's not my secret to tell."

"Candy?" Julia urged. "I already know about that."

"Well, I didn't," Alfie said as he reached for the door. "If he was sleeping with Candy, that's not what I'm talking about. I should go. I have an early start tomorrow. Thanks again for inviting me."

With that, Alfie opened the door and walked off

into the night. Julia watched as he secured his helmet over his head before climbing onto his motorbike. After revving the engine, he turned the bike around in the tight lane and sped off out of sight.

"That was a weird evening," Barker whispered, appearing behind her with a glass of wine. "At least they get on. They're like two peas in a pod."

"Yeah," Julia said absentmindedly as she accepted the wine. "He just told me Shane was having an affair with someone else."

"Who?"

"He wouldn't say." Julia paused to sip her wine. "Said it's not his secret to tell. He's giving me a weird feeling. I can't help but feel like he's connected to the Shane case."

Barker pulled Julia through to the kitchen where he unlocked his briefcase. He pulled out the piece of paper he had almost showed her before Alfie arrived.

"I'm glad he mentioned his criminal past because this won't come as a shock," Barker said as he handed over the paper. "I got one of the boys to do a search on him when you told me his real name. There's a little more than accidental tourism crime."

CHAPTER 13

The next day in Julia's café, the list of Alfie's criminal convictions dominated her thoughts. Along with his arrests in other countries that he had touched on, his past was littered with criminal activity dating back to his early teens.

From shoplifting, breaking and entering, car theft, and everything in between, it seemed Alfie had been involved in petty crime for most of his life, even if Julia would not have suspected such a life for someone who came across as so kind. As Barker had tried to reassure her, none of the charges had been serious enough to send him to prison, but his most recent conviction was a year-old assault charge. She was trying her best to not judge Alfie based on the information she had read, but as the day passed, it was becoming more and more difficult to ignore the facts.

"He's here!" Jessie cried, running out of the kitchen when Alfie pulled up outside on his motorbike. "See you later. I don't know what time I'll be home."

"Keep your phone on," Julia called to her. "And stay safe!"

Jessie waved that she would before opening the café door. She took in Alfie's motorbike before accepting a spare helmet and jumping on the back. Alfie waved into the café at Julia before riding off.

Now that she was alone, Julia flipped the sign from '*OPEN*' to '*CLOSED*' before pulling up a chair. With a slice of leftover cheesecake and a cup of peppermint and liquorice tea, she opened her laptop and started a search for '*Alfred Rice*'.

Nearly an hour later, the sun had set, and she had a folder on her laptop filled with news articles detailing Alfie's different arrests. As Barker had said, none of them seemed all that serious, but the sheer volume of them worried her, even if the main concentration had happened during his teenage years. She looked down at her list of suspects in her ingredients notepad and drew a circle around his name.

"What are you still doing here?" Dot cried as she hurried into the café in a flurry of wind. "I saw your light from across the village green and thought you might be being burgled."

"Curtain twitching again, Gran?" Julia replied with a chuckle as she closed the laptop. "I was just looking at something. It's a long story. Oh, you won't even know about Jessie's brother, will you?"

"Jessie's *what*?" Dot cried, pulling up the chair across from Julia. "Tell me *everything*!"

Julia spent the next thirty minutes telling Dot as much as she knew. She gasped and asked questions in the right places, but for the most part, she let Julia talk her through the story, right up to what she had just spent the past hour doing.

"Never trust a man with that many tattoos!" Dot exclaimed finally. "Makes me wonder about what they are trying to cover up!"

"The most confusing part is that I really liked

him," Julia said as she circled his name once more in her notepad. "I still *do* like him. He's sweet and considerate, and he's been through a lot, just like Jessie, but -"

"He gives you a bad feeling?" Dot jumped in with a knowing nod as she pushed her curls up at the back. "Say no more. Us South girls have always had strong women's intuition, and yours is especially powerful. You could put Evelyn out of business if you switched gears. When has your gut ever led you wrong, dear? In all of these cases, when has it ever been wrong?"

Julia could think of many times she had got things wrong or misunderstood situations, but this felt different. There was so much clouding her judgement that she did not know what her gut was saying. Worst of all, she had a small voice in the back of her head telling her that she was only suspicious because Jessie had instantly bonded with Alfie, and she hated to think she was that kind of person.

"She's out with him now," Julia said as she pulled her phone from her apron pocket. "They've ridden off on a motorbike somewhere, and I have no idea where they've gone, and as usual, she hasn't texted me."

Julia scrolled through her notifications, a text message from six minutes ago catching her attention. She checked her volume settings, and once again her phone was on silent without her knowing.

"Katie has just texted me."

"Probably some pointless drivel," Dot replied with a waft of her hand. "That woman has a brain like soup. I don't know what your father -"

"It says '*It's all kicking off here! Come quick!*'," Julia read aloud. "Candy Bennett is staying at the manor. I think something's happening."

Dot sprang up from her seat, almost knocking the chair over in the process. She stared expectantly at Julia as she read the message again.

"*Well?*" Dot cried, hands planted on her hips. "What are you waiting for? *Let's go*! We've missed six minutes of the drama already!"

DESPITE DOT'S ENCOURAGEMENT, JULIA managed to stick to the speed limit on their drive up to Peridale Manor. The manor came into view, lights in every window banishing the darkness. When Julia noticed Candy hanging out of one of the upstairs windows, throwing clothes down to the ground, she realised what was going on.

"And I *never* liked the way you dressed!" she

223

screeched down at Harold, who was standing on the gravel in front of the house picking up his things. "You're forty-five, not fifteen! Start dressing your age!"

Julia's father and Katie were in the doorway with baby Vinnie, looking up at Candy, neither of them saying anything.

"After all these years, you do this?" Harold cried up as more of his clothes tumbled to the ground. "After everything I've put up with, *now* is when you call things off? After everything I've ignored, and all the horrible things you've done that I've forgiven, you're the one to turn on me? How does that work, Candice?"

"It's *Candy*!" she cried as she sent a shoe zooming towards him. "And I've wanted to do this for years. You're weak, Harold! You've never been a match for a woman like me!"

Julia killed the engine and carefully climbed out of her car, not wanting to disrupt things too much. Candy vanished from the window before returning with a handful of underwear. She tossed it into the air, and the garments fluttered down to the ground like confetti, covering the pink and black Range Rovers in the process. Harold hurried to gather them, embarrassment evident on his face.

"*You*!" Candy screeched, pointing at Julia. "Why are *you* always popping up? You're like a bad smell!"

"Excuse me?" Julia's father, Brian, called, stepping out to look up at Candy. "Julia is my daughter, and she's welcome here. You, young lady, are not! I want you to leave my house this instant!"

"*Brian*!" Katie called, stepping out to pull him back. "Let's just stay out of it."

"This is really big of you, Candice," Harold cried as he gathered up the last of his clothes. "I should have left you years ago. I was clinging on to a tiny shred of you that I thought was still in there, but Candice has been gone for years. Candy has well and truly taken over. Enjoy your next fling with the next poor builder who comes your way."

"Oh, get over yourself, Harold!" Candy cried as she lobbed another shoe at him. "I married you because you were safe, but I realised I didn't want safe. I wanted exciting, and your idea of exciting is watching an old sci-fi movie you've seen a hundred times. They're for kids, Harold! Grow up!"

"You grow up!" he called back. "I can't believe I've put up with your rubbish for all these years. It's a shame Shane is dead because you'd make a great couple."

"So what?" Candy shrieked as she clung to the

edge of the window. "I slept with the builder! Why don't you remind me again? Who cares? He *excited* me! He knew how to make me feel good, Harold. That's more than I can ever say about you. You're a pathetic little man, and I should have done this a long time ago!"

Julia heard a clicking noise coming from the bushes next to the cars, and it seemed Harold did at the same time. He marched over and pulled out a man with a long-lens camera. He looked to be as old as Julia's father and shocked to have been dragged out of his hiding spot.

"Really classy, Candice!" Harold called up as he held the back of the man's jacket. "Hiring a leech to capture the breakdown of our marriage? Are you that desperate for the media attention? They don't care about you anymore. The soaps don't want you, the movies don't want you, and the theatre companies don't want you, and I'm not surprised! You're a diva, and nobody likes a diva! The most you're going to get from now on are reality TV shows and Christmas pantomimes, and it's what you deserve!"

The photographer snapped a close-up shot of Harold's face before Harold threw the man to the ground. Candy squeaked, and Julia expected another barrage of insults to come, but she slammed the window shut instead. Brian tossed Harold a roll of black bags before retreating into the house with Katie and Vinnie. Dot, who had been watching everything unfold from the car, looked disappointed that the fight was over.

Without asking if her help was needed, Julia began helping Harold stuff his clothes into the bags.

"Thank you," he said as he looked up at the window where Candy had been. "I guess all women aren't so bad."

"Not even half of us," Julia replied with a friendly smile. "Can I drive you anywhere? The B&B in town should have a room free if you want somewhere to lay your head for the night. Evelyn is lovely."

Without replying, Harold nodded and carried his bags towards Julia's car. The photographer continued to snap pictures, but Harold was either used to it or did not care about his private life being captured so brutally.

After squashing the bags into the boot of the car, Harold climbed into the backseat. He took his glasses off and rubbed them on the edge of his t-shirt before letting out an exhausted sigh.

"What happened tonight?" Julia asked, looking at him in the rear-view mirror. "Do you think it's over for good?"

"There's no going back after that," Harold said as he slid his glasses back on. "We started arguing about the house again. I told her I was going to pull my money out of it because I was tired of being pushed around. I don't even know why I agreed to build it in the first place. Candy's always had a way of getting what she wanted, but I knew this build was cursed from the moment she thought of it. I think she convinced herself that moving to the countryside was the right thing for her career. Maybe she thought she'd be the star of the village and rebuild from here, but the shine always wears off when people see the real her. She's finished in the business, and she knows it. She's burned most of her bridges with her attitude. I've overheard the conversations she's been having with her agent recently. She's being offered bit-parts in adverts and low rent reality gigs. Without me propping her up, her life will crumble within weeks. Her money is drying up faster than she realises."

"Who would have known?" Dot muttered with a slight smirk, no doubt already trying to figure out who she was going to call first with the gossip. "How the mighty have fallen, eh?"

Deciding now was not the right time to pry,

Julia put her car into reverse, spun around, and set off back towards the village. During the drive, she glanced at Harold through the mirror, but he looked like he had nothing left to give. When they pulled up outside the B&B, Dot jumped out and immediately scurried back to her cottage.

"I'll help you in with your bags," Julia said as she pulled her keys from the ignition. "Evelyn is a friend of mine. I'll make sure she looks after you."

With the black bags in hand, they walked up to the B&B. After ringing the musical doorbell, Evelyn's grandson, Mark, answered the door. He was dressed as though he was about to head out, in skin-tight ripped black jeans, a hooded denim jacket, and a t-shirt for a band Julia did not recognise. His black hair was straightened over his eyes, which were circled in his usual liner.

"Good evening," Mark said shyly as he looked down at the bags in their hands. "Do you need a room?"

"Just a single," Julia explained. "Harold needs somewhere to stay for tonight."

"You're in luck," Mark said as he pushed the door open. "We only have one room available."

As Julia followed Harold into the sweet-scented hallway, she realised the empty room had likely belonged to Shane. She wondered why she had not asked to look at the place before, not that she expected she would find anything left behind that the police had not already seen, and that Evelyn had not cleaned up.

"First door on the first floor," Mark said as he passed a key to Harold. "Nan is just in the bath, but I've made a note of you, so you can pay tomorrow morning. Breakfast is at half eight, and complimentary tarot readings are at nine."

Harold accepted the key before heading up the narrow staircase to the first floor. He walked straight up to the first door, unlocked it and headed inside. Still holding one of his black bags, Julia hurried up after him, hovering on the spot where Shane had pinned Alfie against the wall.

"Is this what my life will become?" Harold sat as he looked around the eccentrically decorated room. "B&Bs and going broke?"

Julia closed the door and put the bag with the others. She turned on the bedside lamps before closing the curtains for him. She sat on the edge of the bed and patted next to her for him to join her.

"I thought you made good money from coding?" Julia asked as she looked around the room, which was decorated with clashing earth-tone prints and trinkets from around the world. "You can survive without Candy. I've been there. I know what it's like to start all over again."

"Did your divorce bankrupt you?" Harold asked as he took his glasses off to rub between his eyes. "I know Candy. She's going to come after everything I have. She'll hide the little money she has left, and she'll find a way to take the clothes off my back. She won't stop until I'm left with nothing."

"Is that why you've stayed with her for all this time?"

Harold shrugged as he pushed his glasses back up his nose. He looked at Julia with a sad smile, letting her know there was more to it than that.

"I really did love her," he whispered, his voice cracking. "For all her faults, I loved her. When I found out about Shane, I was broken. She went out during the day on Valentine's Day to meet up with the builder to talk things over, and she never came home. I knew what she was doing. When she came back, I tried to confront her, and she left. I just went to bed and ignored it. She went out again the day after and met him here at the B&B. I waited outside until she came out, and it was obvious what they had done. I wasn't even surprised. But when I told her that I knew, something changed within me. I didn't want to just sit down and take any of this anymore. I fought back, so she slapped me hard, and then she ran out. Since that day, I kept pushing back and fighting my corner, and she didn't like it. Tonight, she finally got to feel what it was like to be in my shoes. I was the one shouting at her, and she didn't like it. She kicked me out and started throwing my clothes out of the window. I bet she thought she was trying to teach me a lesson, but I'm done. We're over. I'm not covering for her anymore. Did you know I was her alibi the night of Shane's murder? I told the police she was at home with me all night. They found her DNA all over him, and they had it on file after she was caught shoplifting an expensive necklace last year. She begged me to lie for her, so I did. She wouldn't tell me what she'd really been doing, but I knew by that point. I think she thought I was oblivious to it all, but I knew everything. I told them we were at the manor all night in the bedroom while I was working. I showed them my work log, so they could see the timestamps, but that only covered me. The truth is, she left around half five, and she didn't come back until the early hours of the morning. I don't know what she was up to. I can't even say she didn't kill the man. Maybe it would be better for me if she had. She can't take all my money from behind bars."

"Do you think she would be capable of something like that?" Julia asked carefully, her heart racing. "Capable of murder?"

Harold stared into her eyes, a sad smile on his face.

"I don't know that woman," he replied flatly. "I don't know what she's capable of."

Heavy footsteps raced up the staircase, shaking the floorboards in the bedroom. They ran along the hallway, slamming a door behind them. Julia looked at Harold and then down at the bags. She knew he would land on his feet somehow, and she definitely knew his life would improve without Candy in it.

"I think you should tell the police you got your alibi wrong," Julia said. "Even if she's innocent, establishing a real timeline might lead them to the real killer. Tell them you mixed up the days and you're sorry. You're not going to get in trouble."

Harold nodded that he would as he slid his glasses back on. When he looked up at Julia, she saw a glimmer of hope in his eyes.

"Why are you so nice to me?" Harold asked. "You barely know me."

"Because I once had a Candy in my life too," Julia said as she looked down at her pearl engagement ring. "And now I have a Barker. Find your Barker, Harold. You deserve it."

Leaving Harold to settle into his new room, Julia walked towards the door. When she heard the heavy footsteps walking back across the hallway, she paused and listened for them to pass.

"I don't care," she heard a familiar voice say as they hurried past. "I need money, and I need it now! Do you want me to go to the police about what I saw you doing with Shane? I'm sure they'd want to speak to you if I did, and I know you don't want that."

Julia pulled open the door and watched Alfie hurry down the stairs, a large black bag slung over his shoulder. When he reached the bottom of the stairs, he paused and listened to the person on the other side of the phone.

"I don't care what you're going through," he snarled down the phone. "Get whatever you can together and meet me at the building site in half an hour. I'm leaving Peridale tonight."

Alfie ended the call and stuffed his phone into his pocket. Julia could not help but fly down the stairs after him, blocking the front door before he could reach it.

"Where are you going, Alfie?" she asked, her

voice shaking. "Why are you in such a rush?"

"Please don't make this any harder than it needs to be," Alfie said with a heavy sigh. "I'm leaving Peridale tonight, and Jessie is coming with me. I'm all she has, and we're going to see the world together."

"Has she agreed to that?"

"We talked about it tonight," Alfie said, his dark eyes staring deep into Julia's. "I realised I needed to seize the day. Spending time alone with her tonight, I realised how much I'd missed. We need to do this. You've done a great job with her, but it's my turn now. I can make up for not being there for all those years. I need to."

"Who was that on the phone?" Julia asked. "Who are you blackmailing?"

Alfie gritted his jaw, and for a moment, Julia was not sure what he was capable of. Even though fear bubbled deep inside, she held her ground and did not move.

"Please, Julia," Alfie whispered, his eyes begging her to move. "You don't understand."

"No, it's *you* who doesn't understand," Julia snapped back. "I've known Jessie for a year, and you've known her for a couple of days. Peridale is her home, and she won't agree to leave it just because you say so."

"She already has."

The shock of Alfie's confession loosened Julia's arm enough for him to push past and open the door. She looked on dumbfounded as he ran to his motorbike. Without putting on a helmet, he sped off into the village.

"What a lovely surprise!" Evelyn called from the top of the stairs as she walked down in a fluffy dressing gown, a towel holding back her wet hair. "Can I interest you in a cup of tea?"

Julia stared dead ahead at the reception desk at the end of the hall as her mind raced. She pulled her phone out of her pocket and dialled Jessie's number. It rang and rang, but there was no answer.

"Jessie, it's Julia," she said after the voicemail signal beeped. "Please call me. Don't leave things like this. I love you."

Julia pushed the phone into her pocket and then pushed her fingers up into her hair.

"What's happened, dear?" Evelyn cooed as she hurried over to wrap a hand around Julia's shoulders. "Come and sit down. You look like you've just had the worst news of your life."

"I think I might have," Julia replied, her voice not sounding like her own.

Evelyn led her into the dimly lit sitting room and placed Julia on the couch in the middle of the room. Without saying another word, Evelyn scurried off to the kitchen, no doubt to make them a pot of tea.

Julia stared at the wooden tarot boxes on the coffee table, unsure of what was happening. She felt like she was in a nightmare, stuck to Evelyn's couch and unable to move. She forced herself to stand up and she turned to the door, but her brain would not function. Where was Jessie and was she really about to leave her?

Her mind emptied when her eyes wandered to something hanging from a string next to the door. Just like they had at the building site in the rain, the plastic-covered red roses called to her, drawing her in.

"*Evelyn*?" Julia called. "Where did you get these roses?"

Julia crept towards them, the buds crinkled, and the plastic stained with water marks. Hidden between the stems, Julia spotted a ruined piece of card, the ink and paper now one gloopy mess.

"Oh, I found them in the outside bin," Evelyn replied as she hurried into the room with a rattling tray of tea. "It's amazing what people will throw away these days. Probably an unwanted Valentine's gift, but I was drawn to them, so I hung them up to dry out. I do love dried flowers, don't you? I didn't want to disrupt the plastic until they'd dried out fully. They were quite soggy."

"What day did you find them?"

"Oh, let me think," Evelyn said as she tapped her chin. "It was night time, and I was putting out the rubbish from the day. I'd waited longer than usual because of the terrible rain we had that day, so it was quite late. I pulled the flowers out, and I looked up at the sky. I remember thinking how beautiful the moon was. It was a waning crescent with - Oh, I don't know - fifteen to seventeen percent visibility? I'm sorry I can't be more specific, but I think it was a Sunday."

"You got all that from the moon?"

"Oh, no, dear," Evelyn said with a chuckle. "I remember making a tofu roast for dinner, and I had quite a lot to throw away. Turns out builders aren't too fond of my non-meat menu. Yes, the Sunday with the rain."

Julia knew exactly what day she was talking about. It was the day she had visited the manor for a playdate between Pearl, Dottie, and Vinnie, and the same day she had caught Alfie staring into the rain at the building site where she later spotted the elusive roses.

"I know who did it," Julia whispered, her eyes widening as she stared at Evelyn. "How could I have missed this? Of course, it all comes down to the flowers! I know who murdered Shane and Harriet."

"Who, dear?"

"*Valentine's Day*!" Julia said quickly, her mind slotting the pieces together at lightning speed. "It wasn't who *bought* the flowers, it was who *received* them. I need to go."

"But I made tea!"

"And I'm sure it's delicious," Julia said as she hurried to the front door. "Another time, Evelyn. Thank you! Thank you so much!

CHAPTER 14

J ulia sped through the village, only slowing down as she passed the building site. When she saw that whoever Alfie was planning to meet was not there yet, she continued up to her cottage.

A light drizzle began to fall as she climbed out of the car. It felt like an omen of what was to come, but for now, Julia pushed those thoughts to the back of her mind. The lights in her cottage were on, but Alfie's motorbike was not outside.

"*Jessie?*" Julia cried as she burst through the door. "Jessie, are you here?"

Barker appeared in the dining room door, already in his pyjamas.

"I've been trying to call you," Barker said. "Where have you been? I was starting to get worried."

Julia checked her phone, and once again it was on silent. She shook it before tossing it onto the side table.

"I think it's broken," she said as she looked desperately around the cottage. "Where's Jessie? Has Alfie already come? Barker, please tell me -"

"Where's the fire?" Jessie said as she pulled open her bedroom door. "I'm right here. What's going on?"

Julia wasted no time grabbing Jessie in a hug. She did not want to let go, but Jessie wriggled away like Mowgli the one time Julia had tried to bath him.

"Alright, cake lady," Jessie said as she looked down her nose. "Chill out. Are you sure you're not going through menopause? You're acting super weird lately."

"You're still here," Julia said as she held Jessie's arms. "He's probably coming to pick you up after he's got the money. You need to listen to me, Jessie. I know Alfie seems nice, and he is, but there's more to him than you know. He has a past - a *criminal* past. You can't go with him like this. You can't just run away with him because he's asked you to. You've got a life here. I don't want to lose you like this."

Jessie looked down the hallway to Barker and then to Julia. She arched a brow as she took a step back, her hands up.

"Woah, cake lady!" Jessie cried as she stepped back into her bedroom. "What are you talking about? I'm not going anywhere."

"But Alfie said -"

"Alfie said what?" Jessie jumped in. "When did you talk to him?"

"Just now at the B&B. He thinks you're running away together. He's packed a bag, and I think he's coming to get you. He said you'd agreed to it."

"I agreed to travel with him for a *holiday*," Jessie said, taking another step back. "I said it would be cool to go somewhere together, but I didn't mean right now. I'm not running away. This is my home."

"But -"

"But you just thought I would run away like that?" Jessie quipped, her tone twisting Julia's heart. "Don't you know me?"

"I -"

"And to use Alfie's past against him like that?" Jessie jumped in again. "He told me everything tonight. We went out to dinner, and he told me every gritty detail. It's not like I had a clean record before coming here. Would you use that against me if you needed to? I thought you were better than that."

"Julia was just worried about you," Barker said, stepping forward to join Julia by her side. "We both were. We just want the best for you. We wanted to know what Alfie's intentions were."

"His *intentions*?" Jessie forced a laugh as she shook her head. "You don't have to do this. I don't need you to play the parent game, I just need you to be real with me. I'm eighteen in a couple of months. I'm not a little girl. I've just found out I have a brother and you both jump on him like Mowgli on catnip? He's not perfect, but am I? Look at that locket, Julia. I came into your life by breaking into your café. What if this was flipped and Alfie was your foster son? Would I have been the villain because I'd done bad things? Not cool, guys. Not cool at all."

Julia felt herself shrinking into invisibility. She rested her hand on the locket, knowing everything

Jessie had just said was right.

"I just don't want to lose you," Julia said, the words choking her. "And I - I was worried that -"

"I'm not going anywhere," Jessie whispered, stepping forward and pulling Julia into a hug. "Just calm down, okay? If Alfie wants to run away, then that's what he wants to do. He knows where I live. I'm not running away from the thing I've been looking for since I was a kid. Alfie is my brother, but you two are - you're -"

"Barker and Julia," Barker jumped in. "The two adults who should trust you a little more to make grownup decisions."

"I like that you worry about me," Jessie said, her voice retreating to that of a little girl. "But you can trust me. I'm not as reckless as you think I am. I wouldn't throw all of this away to see the world, and if I did ever go out there, I'd do it with a return ticket already booked."

"I'm sorry," Julia said, the words catching in her throat. "Can you tell I'm still trying to get to grips with this parenting thing?"

"Yes," Jessie said with a chuckle. "But the less you try, the better you are at it. What was the rush, anyway? Alfie only dropped me off fifteen minutes ago. I doubt he was zooming back to whisk me away. He could have done that earlier."

Julia checked her watch, the meeting deadline for Alfie's blackmail victim creeping closer.

"I think I know who killed Shane and Harriet," Julia said carefully. "I'll explain everything, but I think I'm going to need both of you to help."

TWENTY MINUTES LATER, JULIA WALKED alone to the building site down the lane. The metal structure looked less like a house than ever, but she assumed that was the intention behind the design. Even in the dark, it was an ugly structure that had no place in Peridale, especially when she remembered who owned the land.

She checked her watch; she was right on time. When she reached the edge of the garden wall, she hung back, blending into the shadows behind a lamppost. Orange light flooded the concrete and metal space as the rain pattered softly from the jet-black sky. As expected, her main suspect was waiting in the middle of the structure, their head protected from the downpour by a hood.

Many would have rushed forward knowing what Julia knew, but she hung back until she heard the roar of Alfie's motorbike making its way up the winding lane. The hooded figure turned around to face the bright headlights as Alfie pulled up only metres away from Julia. Luckily for her, she was well hidden in the shadows, and Alfie was too preoccupied with his cobbled-together plan.

"You came," Alfie said as he unclipped the gate and walked towards the shadowy figure. "Did you get me some money?"

"Do you think this is a game?" they hissed in reply. "You can't just expect me to pull up money because you asked for it. I'm broke, Alfie! I don't have a penny to my name, and I don't think for a minute you'll tell the police about what you saw. You know as well as I do that it doesn't mean anything."

"Do I?" Alfie replied abruptly. "I'm not playing around either. I'm doing the right thing for once. I need something to get away, so I can start a new life for my sister and me. You must have something."

"Do you want to check my pockets?" they cried. "*Here*! Have my watch. What about my ring?" They tossed the items onto the ground. "Does this make you feel big to blackmail someone when they're at rock bottom? I have nothing to give you!"

Alfie scooped up the ring and the watch, pocketing them after checking them over. He seemed satisfied, but he did not immediately head back to his motorbike.

"I need cash too," Alfie said. "I won't be able to pawn these until the morning. You must have something."

"Don't push it, Alfie," they cried, their finger extending. "I like you, but don't push me. You don't know what I'm capable of."

Julia stepped from her hiding place and slipped through the open gate. Neither of them noticed her creep towards them, both preoccupied with staring the other down.

"He might not know what you're capable of," Julia started, her voice loud and clear, "but I do, Mikey."

The architect ripped back his hood, his platinum blond buzz cut shining ethereally in the darkness. He squinted at Julia as the rain intensified and dribbled down his face.

"What is this?" Mikey cried, looking at Alfie. "Double teaming? I thought better of you, Julia. I thought you were nice. You know I'm broke. I told you everything."

"Yes, you did," Julia said with a nod as she considered her approach. "I just needed a few more pieces to see the bigger picture. After you told me about your heartbreak with your ex-husband, I urged you to not give up on love, but you told me you'd found someone and that it had ended. I didn't realise you meant you'd ended Shane's life."

Alfie glanced down at Julia, looking as uncomfortable as Mikey did, but from the lack of shock in his gaze, she knew he had figured it out too.

"You hear about people so unable to accept their true selves that they resent the very thing that makes them unique," Julia continued as the rain soaked through her coat. "I can't imagine it was easy for Shane coming to terms with being gay, which explains why he lashed out and called people '*queer*' every chance he got. It was a defence mechanism. He was saying '*look over there because there's nothing to see here*', but you saw everything, didn't you, Alfie? That's why we're here tonight. The day I was at the B&B delivering a cake for Evelyn, you walked in on Shane and Mikey in bed together, and your boss was so horrified that his secret might get out, he didn't even bother putting clothes on before threatening you. If only the door had been a little more open, I might have seen you, Mikey, and you might not have had to kill Harriet too. Of course, this is only a theory, but neither of you are jumping in to tell me how wrong I've got things."

"I - I - I -" Mikey stuttered. "You're -"

"*Right,*" Alfie jumped in. "She's right. That's exactly what I saw, but I didn't say anything because I didn't want to believe you were involved in his death. I thought you knew already, Julia. When we talked in the pub before I saw your locket, I thought you were talking about Mikey and Shane, but you must have been talking about his divorce. When you asked me again in the hall at your cottage yesterday, I realised you didn't know after all, and that's when I realised I still had a bargaining chip if I needed to use it. The police didn't want to talk to you, so I left it alone."

"Until you realised you could use it to get something you wanted," Julia said with a sigh. "Two wrongs don't make a right, Alfie, but I understand where you're coming from. I even understand where you're coming from, Mikey. It couldn't have been easy to be rejected like that, which is why you killed Shane?"

"What do you know?" Mikey snapped before spitting at Julia's feet. "You're just a little café owner."

"I know that your divorce broke you and that you were looking for love wherever you could find it," Julia continued. "You told me very early on that you'd worked with Shane on many projects before. If Shane was really as hateful as he came across, I doubt someone like you would keep him around, even if he was the best builder in the world. I just didn't see it at first because it was the furthest thing from my mind, but when I saw the flowers again - the flowers Shane bought for *you* as an apology - everything clicked. Where did Shane spend Valentine's Day, Mikey?"

The question caused Mikey's sharp jawline to tighten.

"With *her*," Mikey snarled. "With that woman. Candy marked him the second she saw him. I tried to tell her to stay away, but she didn't listen. I loved Shane, and she just wanted a new plaything. The only reason I even agreed to come to Peridale before the build started was to be in the same place as Shane for Valentine's Day. We'd been seeing each other for almost a year. It was going to be the first holiday we'd spent together, but he spent it with her."

"And that's why he sent you the flowers," Julia jumped back in. "The card said '*I'm sorry. I love you*'. I assumed the card had been written by someone apologising for killing Shane, but I was wrong there. I saw the flowers right where we're standing now.

You left them right where you killed him."

"I didn't *leave* them here," Mikey scoffed with a shake of his head. "I *threw* them over the garden wall in a fit of rage. I spent a whole year trying to get him to accept himself, so we could be open and live our lives, but he wouldn't be a man and admit who he really was. He ran back to women like he was proving something to himself. He broke my heart over and over, and I let him because I wanted my second shot at happiness. I thought if I gave him enough time, he'd come around but -"

"You realised he'd never come around," Julia said, her heart aching for Mikey. "He might have apologised with the flowers and professed his love, but he saw her again, didn't he? In fact, I know he did. After he ran out on you in the B&B, he met up with Candy the night you killed him."

"When he'd finished with her, he called me crying, admitting his love again," Mikey said, his tone mocking. "I was tired of it! I couldn't do it anymore! I wanted to be happy, not to keep living behind lies. I just wanted the happy ending that I deserved. He begged me to meet up with him, but I didn't want to go. If he hadn't cried over the phone, he might still be alive, but it broke my heart to hear him sobbing my name, so I met him. We went for a burger out of the village, and then we came here to talk away from prying eyes. It was going well at first, but I gave him an ultimatum. I told him he'd have to end things with Candy for good and out our relationship to the world. I wanted him to do it the next day at the building site. He laughed in my face. He told me I was crazy, and that it was never going to happen. He said I was his little secret, and that's how it was going to stay. I felt so cheap and dirty. I realised nothing I could do or say would change him. So - so I - so I -"

"Picked up the nearest brick and hit him," Alfie whispered, the words heavy. "Oh, Mikey. I thought you were one of the good ones."

"I didn't mean to *kill* him!" Mikey cried, tears collecting across his thick lash line. "I just wanted to hurt him, but there was so much blood. I panicked, and I ran, and I kept quiet. I thought if I got on with my work and I kept my head down, it would go away, but Candy was relentless. She kept picking and picking at me, and it drove me insane. It's like she knew what had happened. She didn't even seem upset about his death. He was just her toy. I loved him. I never wanted to kill him."

"But, you did want to murder Harriet," Julia said, her heart heavy. "She was my friend, and you stabbed her in the neck. I visited her about the flowers you left. She claimed not to know who had left them, but I think I put a bug in her mind. That's what Harriet was like. Did she figure it out?"

"She called me when I was at the pub with you," Mikey continued, his eyes glazing over as he stared through Julia. "I ran to the bathroom to throw up, and an unknown number called. I thought it might be one of the suppliers, so I answered. When I realised who it was, I thought she must have seen the flowers. They were only here for about an hour. I came right back and got rid of them, but you must have seen them first. If you hadn't gone to her, she wouldn't have figured it out. Shane went to the shop and bought the flowers with cash. I doubt she knew who he was then, but I suppose him manhandling her at the demolition a week later shook the memory loose. Shane didn't want to be seen with the flowers, so he paid her to deliver them. He gave my number as the contact. She delivered them to me at the B&B. When she called me, she said '*you're the architect*'. I guess my voice gave it away. It's not like I sound like most other men, is it? She told me to meet her at her shop, so I went to see what she knew. She had most of the pieces, and I knew she'd figure it out soon enough, so I did what I had to."

"You stabbed her in the neck with her gardening scissors?" Julia whispered as she pushed her wet hair from her face. "You didn't need to do that. I can understand your motive for killing Shane, but Harriet deserved better."

"I fell in too deep," Mikey cried, the rain on his cheeks looking like tears. "I couldn't stop it. I've come too far to go to prison for this. I won't last two minutes. You can't make me."

With that, Mikey burst forward and pushed Julia into Alfie. They both tumbled backwards, falling with a thud on the wet concrete foundation. Julia scrambled to her feet before helping Alfie up, but Mikey was already sprinting away to the back of the plot.

"We should chase him!" Alfie cried. "He killed two people!"

"Just wait," Julia whispered as she shielded her eyes from the rain. "I had a feeling this would happen."

Just like clockwork, Jessie and Barker appeared from the dark bushes at the back of the plot. Mikey ground to a halt, unsure of which way to turn. Jessie advanced first, followed quickly by Barker who overtook her. He dove onto the slender architect, knocking him clean off his feet in what looked like the world's most unfair game of rugby ever.

"*DS Christie*?" Julia called out, not needing to look over her shoulder. "I really hope you're waiting with the handcuffs."

The creak of the gate let her know her quickly cobbled together plan had worked flawlessly.

"I hate it when you're right," DS Christie mumbled as he walked past. "Let's get this over with."

"You did an excellent job of creeping up the lane," Julia called after him as she looked at the two police cars parked silently in the dark lane behind them. "Points for keeping the headlights off."

Barker held Mikey securely while DS Christie attached the handcuffs, the rain lashing down around them. As he read Mikey his rights, he dragged him towards the gate where a uniformed officer was waiting to open the door. When Mikey was securely in the back of the car, Julia finally let go of the breath she had been holding.

"Any more funny business like that, and I'll make sure you live to regret it," Julia whispered to Alfie out of the corner of her mouth as Jessie and Barker walked over arm in arm. "Do you understand me, Alfred?"

"Loud and clear, cake lady," he replied. "Jessie

was right when she said you could be scary."

Julia grinned at Alfie, and he grinned back. Deep down, she knew she had nothing to worry about.

"That was ace!" Jessie called into the rain, her dark hair stuck to her face. "He went down like a bowling pin! Alright, bro."

"Alright, sis."

"I heard you were going to kidnap me."

"Something along those lines," Alfie replied uneasily. "I had a mad moment."

"It's cool," Jessie replied, nudging him with her arm. "You'll get used to those in this family. Have you met Dot yet?"

Jessie looped her arm through Alfie's, and they set off towards the gate, chatting into the rain as though they had never been separated a single day in their lives.

"What happens now?" Barker asked, shielding his eyes as the police car sped back down the lane. "I'm not used to being on this side of the law."

"There's only one thing to do," Julia said, wrapping her hand around Barker's before following Jessie and Alfie towards the gate. "We go home and have hot chocolate and a cupcake."

CHAPTER 15

W ork on the building site ceased the next day with Candy officially ending the project. No one was sure if it was because her architect had been charged on two counts of murder or because she was about to start a costly divorce, but no one seemed especially sad about the news.

Harold checked out of the B&B before breakfast, skipping his complimentary tarot reading.

He did not stop by the manor nor did he leave a forwarding address. Julia hoped wherever he had gone that he would carve a new life for himself like she had once had to do.

Candy, who was still hiding at the manor, had yet to show her face in the village. Word of her involvement with Shane had spread like wildfire, not just around Peridale, but across the internet too. Pictures of her throwing Harold's clothes out of the window had been uploaded next to headlines featuring words such as '*psychotic*', '*washed-up*', '*bitter*', and '*irrelevant*'. Even if she decided to stay in Peridale, the shine had definitely dulled on her star, and Julia suspected it would not be long before her father and Katie gave her an official marching order. A small part of Julia knew that Candy would love the attention.

Just like after any significant event in the village, Julia's café became the central point of gossip for all who wanted to indulge. Dot held court, recounting her discovery of the body, and Julia's final confrontation with Mikey. Both stories had been heavily embellished, but Julia quite liked the part in Dot's story where Julia fought off Mikey with expert karate moves not seen since Bruce Lee himself.

When the café finally quietened down, Billy

walked in with his tail between his legs. To Julia's delight, their awkward argument at dinner was already a distant memory for Jessie.

"Before you try to apologise, don't," Jessie demanded before pecking Billy on the cheek. "I get it, okay? Turns out you were sort of right. I've got some cupcake deliveries if you want to help out? Not quite what you were on at the building site, but it pays."

"Sure, babe," Billy said with a relieved smile. "But I doubt I'll see any of that money. They never paid me a penny."

"Leave it to me," Julia assured him. "I'll have a word with Candy myself. I'm sure she doesn't want the press to hear about how I was witness to her tax avoidance cash-in-hand employment scheme. You'll get your money."

Now that he was officially back at work, Barker walked into the café dressed once more in one of his usual suits. Julia pushed forward the slice of chocolate cake she had already cut for him and got to work making his Americano with an extra shot.

"Hectic day," Barker said as he sat down in the seat across from Dot. "Murder cases bring out the worst in everyone. I picked a bad day to go back."

"Well, if your book takes off, you won't have to

slog it out for much longer," Dot announced before pouring herself another cup of tea from her pot. "You'll both be living in the lap of luxury. Don't forget who your first fan was when you're a millionaire."

"You're a fan of my book?" Barker asked sceptically. "I didn't know you'd read it."

"Well, I haven't," Dot replied as she pushed her curls up. "Not technically. It's not even out yet, but Julia gave me the highlights, and it didn't sound entirely awful. I'm waiting for the book-on-tape version. I don't have the attention span for reading these days. I'm much more a woman of the spoken word."

"Especially when it comes to gossip," Julia said as she passed Barker his coffee. "Do you know when Harriet's funeral is?"

"This Tuesday," Dot exclaimed as though it had slipped her mind. "I wonder who'll do the flowers for it?"

Julia and Barker both gave her the exact same look before they both rolled their eyes.

"Well, I'm only saying what everyone is thinking!" Dot cried. "We're without a florist now. Give it another couple of years, and Peridale will be like every other town in this country. Every shop will either be selling pasties, phones, or things for a pound. Mark my words, Julia! Gentrification is coming, and we must stop it!"

"For once, Gran, I might agree with you," Julia said as she thought about the cold, metal structure that was even more unsightly than Barker's half-destroyed cottage. "I like our little village just the way it is, and next time another actress rolls around, I might sign that petition."

Jessie pushed Billy through the pink beads, a stack of white boxes covering his face. He made his way awkwardly around the counter as Jessie thrust him forward.

"Say it back to me!" Jessie exclaimed. "I want it perfect this time."

"Angel cakes for Malcolm," Billy mumbled from behind the boxes. "And custard slices for Amy?"

"*No!*" Jessie cried. "C'mon, Billy. You're almost as bad as Julia, and she's -"

Before Jessie could finish her sentence, the bell above the café jingled, and Alfie stepped in, wearing the same biker outfit he had worn the day he first arrived in Peridale. His bike was parked exactly where it had been, his large bag strapped to the back of it.

"Evelyn let me check out a little later," Alfie said

sheepishly as he looked around the café. "I guess that makes me homeless."

"Does that mean you're leaving?" Jessie asked, her eyes on the bike outside. "Where will you go?"

Alfie looked back at his bike and then at Jessie before turning to Julia; she could sense what was coming next.

"Actually, sis, I was going to ask if I could crash on your floor until I get on my feet?" he asked, his smile wide but his voice faltering. "I hate to ask, but I wasn't expecting this job to get cut short so quickly, and I only got paid for the first week, so -"

"Of course you can," Julia jumped in before he started begging. "I was going to offer anyway."

"No, no, no!" Dot announced, standing up dramatically, her eyes trained on Alfie. "Jessie is my sort-of-great-granddaughter, which means you're my sort-of-not-quite-great-grandson. I won't have you sleeping on a floor or Julia's lumpy couch when I have two perfectly decent empty bedrooms. They might need some updating, but you're more than welcome to take your pick."

"Like a lodger?" Alfie asked, folding his leather-clad arms across his chest. "Are you sure about that? I wouldn't be able to pay you anything until I get a job."

"Then it's a good thing I know how to stretch my pension," Dot said, walking over to loop her arm through Alfie's. "And before you ask, no I won't cook your meals, I won't wash your underwear, and I don't share the remote control for the television."

"Deal," Alfie said before Dot could change her mind. "Looks like I'm a Peridale resident."

"An unemployed resident," Dot corrected him as she patted him on the chest. "You'll fit right in. C'mon. I'll show you to your room. You can pick between Julia or Sue's old bedrooms. I hope you like pink. They were both going through a phase when it came to buying the wallpaper, but I managed to get a job lot, so it worked out cheaper in the end."

"Alfie?" Billy called as he rested the tall stack of cake boxes on the counter. "If you don't completely hate me already, I might have had an idea about work."

Dot stopped in her tracks and huffed. She swung around, Alfie swinging with her. She rested one hand on her hip, pursed her lips, and waited for Billy to spit out his idea so she could take her 'sort-of-not-quite-great-grandson' home.

"I got the taste for building, and no offence, Jessie, I don't think delivering cupcakes is really my thing," Billy said with an apologetic smile over his shoulder. "I heard something on that business documentary that said you should fill a gap in a market when you see one. I checked the local listings, and I couldn't find any builders still operating in Peridale. You seemed to know what you were doing, and I'm a fast learner."

"You want us to start a business?" Alfie asked, a brow arching. "*Together*?"

"I thought we worked pretty cool together," Billy said with a shrug, his confidence dipping. "We could call it '*Billy and Alfie*' or something. We could start small, doing odd jobs here and there, but if we save up, there's an old builders yard at the bottom of Mulberry Lane that's been sitting empty for the past two years. I reckon we could get a good deal on rent if we haggled. What do you say, mate?"

"Are you being serious?" Alfie laughed with a shake of his head. "'*Billy and Alfie*'? If we're going with anything, it's '*Alfie and Billy*'. That's got more of a ring to it."

"You're in?" Billy asked, the shock obvious. "Like, for real?"

"What have we got to lose?" Alfie replied, wriggling his hand free to hold it out to Billy. "I think we'll make a good team."

They shook hands, both of them grinning like

Cheshire cats.

"Well, now that that's sorted, I've got a crack going up the wall in my kitchen, and I'm pretty sure if it gets any longer my entire cottage is going to fall down," Dot said as she scooped up Billy and Alfie's arms, one on either side. "No time like the present. I want a family discount."

With that, they set off across the village green towards Dot's cottage as the sun shone high in the cloudless sky above them.

"That boy must have really been paying attention to that business documentary," Julia muttered under her breath. "He's cleverer than he looks."

"Not that clever," Jessie moaned as she hurried around the counter. "He's got the keys for my bike lock in his pocket!"

Jessie burst out of the café and ran after them across the village green. As she did, Julia caught sight of the first yellow daffodils of the year peeking up through the flower beds lining the village green.

"Spring is on its way," Julia said, staring at the pretty yellow petals as she rested her head on Barker's. "I think we might have just gained a new family member."

"A toast to our new normal," Barker said as he

lifted his coffee cup in the air. "This is delicious chocolate cake, by the way. Might be your best."

Julia chuckled before kissing Barker on the top of his head. Leaving him to drink his coffee and finish his cake, she resumed her position behind the counter and looked out over the village green. She had a feeling life was not finished with throwing curveballs at her, but she was ready for whatever else was coming her way.

ALSO BY AGATHA FROST

The Scarlet Cove Series
Dead in the Water
Castle on the Hill
Stroke of Death

The Peridale Café Series
Pancakes and Corpses
Lemonade and Lies
Doughnuts and Deception
Chocolate Cake and Chaos
Shortbread and Sorrow
Espresso and Evil
Macarons and Mayhem
Fruit Cake and Fear
Birthday Cake and Bodies
Gingerbread and Ghosts
Cupcakes and Casualties
Blueberry Muffins and Misfortune

If you enjoyed *Cupcakes and Casualties*, why not sign up to Agatha Frost's **FREE** newsletter at **AgathaFrost.com** to hear about brand new releases!

Don't forget to head over to **Amazon** and **Goodreads** to leave a review!

The 12th book in the Peridale Café series is coming May 2018! Julia and friends will be back for another Peridale Cafe Mystery case in *Blueberry Muffins and Misfortune!*

Printed in Great Britain
by Amazon